About Jackie Braun

Jackie Braun is a three-time RITA® Award finalist, a four-time National Readers' Choice Awards finalist and the winner of the Rising Star Award for traditional romantic fiction. She can be reached through her website at www.jackiebraun.com

'"You can't judge a book by its cover." It's an old saying that remains all too true—as Thomas Waverly learns while getting to know Elizabeth Morris.'

—*Jackie Braun*

GW00382962

™

Praise for Jackie Braun

'A great storyline, interesting characters and a fast pace
help immerse readers in this tender tale.'
—RT Book Reviews on
Inconveniently Wed!

'Quite humorous at times, with beautifully written
characters, this is a terrific read.'
—RT Book Reviews on
A Dinner, A Date, A Desert Sheikh

'Solidly plotted, with an edgy, slightly abrasive heroine
and an equally unforgettable hero,
this story is a great read. Don't miss it.'
—RT Book Reviews on
Confidential: Expecting!

'…reading her books [is] a delightful experience that
carries you from laughter to tears and back again.'
—Pink Heart Society on
Boardroom Baby Surprise

The Fiancée Fiasco

Jackie Braun

DID YOU PURCHASE THIS BOOK WITHOUT A COVER?

If you did, you should be aware it is **stolen property** as it was reported *unsold and destroyed* by a retailer. Neither the author nor the publisher has received any payment for this book.

All the characters in this book have no existence outside the imagination of the author, and have no relation whatsoever to anyone bearing the same name or names. They are not even distantly inspired by any individual known or unknown to the author, and all the incidents are pure invention.

All Rights Reserved including the right of reproduction in whole or in part in any form. This edition is published by arrangement with Harlequin Enterprises II BV/S.à.r.l. The text of this publication or any part thereof may not be reproduced or transmitted in any form or by any means, electronic or mechanical, including photocopying, recording, storage in an information retrieval system, or otherwise, without the written permission of the publisher.

This book is sold subject to the condition that it shall not, by way of trade or otherwise, be lent, resold, hired out or otherwise circulated without the prior consent of the publisher in any form of binding or cover other than that in which it is published and without a similar condition including this condition being imposed on the subsequent purchaser.

® and TM are trademarks owned and used by the trademark owner and/or its licensee. Trademarks marked with ® are registered with the United Kingdom Patent Office and/or the Office for Harmonisation in the Internal Market and in other countries.

FFirst published in Great Britain 2012
by Mills & Boon, an imprint of Harlequin (UK) Limited.
Harlequin (UK) Limited, Eton House, 18-24 Paradise Road,
Richmond, Surrey TW9 1SR

© Jackie Braun Fridline 2012

ISBN: 978 0 263 89302 1

Harlequin (UK) policy is to use papers that are natural, renewable and recyclable products and made from wood grown in sustainable forests. The logging and manufacturing process conform to the legal environmental regulations of the country of origin.

Printed and bound in Spain
by Blackprint CPI, Barcelona

Also by Jackie Braun

Confessions of a Girl-Next-Door
Mr Right There All Along
The Road Not Taken
The Princess Next Door
The Daddy Diaries
Inconveniently Wed!
A Dinner, A Date, A Desert Sheikh
Confidential: Expecting!
Boardroom Baby Surprise

Did you know these are also available as eBooks?
Visit www.millsandboon.co.uk

Good things come in threes.
Welcome to the world, Tedder triplets:
Mikenzie, Jameson and Savannah.

CHAPTER ONE

THOMAS Waverly needed a bride.

Time was of the essence, so he couldn't afford to be too picky. Even so, as he mentally thumbed through his little black book, he knew that none of the women he'd dated in the past would do. They would read *way* too much into the situation. They would expect it to be real. But the heirloom diamond engagement ring and all talk of a future wedding would be only for his grandmother's benefit.

Nana Jo was dying.

At least she claimed to be.

Her physician assured Thomas that Josephine O'Keefe was in good health for a woman who'd had a hip replacement the previous year, a brush with breast cancer two decades prior and was now closing in on eighty-one. Her heartbeat could be a bit irregular at times, but medication had been prescribed to take care of that and, according to the doctor, it was. Nana Jo, however, was of another opinion.

She was dying.

It was the dreams, she told Thomas. For the past year, each night as she slumbered, she'd dreamed of her late husband and daughter—Thomas's mother. Nana Jo was sure the dreams were an omen of her own impending death, and nothing Thomas said could convince her otherwise. It was downright unnerving.

The previous Christmas, when he'd made the drive to upstate Michigan to spend the holiday with Nana Jo in her small condo in Charlevoix, she'd told him that the only gift she wanted was to see her only grandchild happily settled before she passed on.

The woman had raised him after a car accident claimed his mother, after which his father had fallen into an alcoholic tailspin. Thomas had been eight, and he'd essentially lost both of his parents. Without hesitation, and despite her own grief, Nana Jo had stepped into the huge void. Instead of enjoying her retirement, she'd taken on full-time parenting. And she'd done an incredible job.

How could he deny her wish? How could he indulge it? It was a no-win situation. So, yes, he'd lied.

He wasn't proud of that. Thomas wasn't one to bend the truth, whether in personal dealings or professional ones, but he would do anything to erase the worry he saw in her eyes. Anything short of actual marriage, that was.

So, even though he was between relationships, he'd said, "I've been seeing someone... special. For several months now, in fact."

The distinction had buoyed Nana Jo's spirits considerably. And no wonder. He'd never dated a woman longer than three months. By that point they were usually expecting things, like an exchange of house keys, a toothbrush in his bathroom and maybe even a drawer of their own in the bureau in his bedroom.

By three months, they were getting clingy, needy. The *L* word, he knew, wouldn't be far behind.

Love. No thank you.

He'd seen firsthand what that four-letter word had done to his father. It had been twenty-seven years since Thomas's mother's death, but Hoyt Waverly still couldn't face life as a widower without a fifth of whiskey handy. Over the years, the brands had become cheaper as Hoyt's finances had deteriorated right along with his health. Today, he was a shell of a man, who only turned up occasionally on Thomas's doorstep and then only because he'd run out of money.

Thomas had no desire to end up like his old man. So, he made a point of ending relationships before three months passed, sometimes before then if the woman started to fall for him a little too hard or too fast.

It wasn't that Thomas was God's gift to women. His ego was healthy, but not overblown. He supposed he was good-looking. Enough of his dates had told him so. And he made a decent living. Not exactly a millionaire since he'd poured so much of his own money into starting his business, but he was plenty comfortable thanks to hard work and some sound investments. Still, the real attribute that seemed to clinch it for him with members of the opposite sex wasn't his looks, his bank account or even, to his chagrin, his skill as a lover. It was his manners.

Apparently, while growing up, he'd paid too close attention to Nana Jo's instructions. She'd insisted that he be polite, chivalrous, attentive and always act interested in other people's opinions and pastimes—even when he wasn't. As a result, over the years a number of women had expressed, covertly at least, their desire to become Mrs. Thomas Waverly. But he wasn't in the market for marriage. Not now. Not ever.

For the past several months, of course, Nana Jo had thought otherwise. To her, special implied altar-bound. He should have corrected her. But she was so happy, so excited. It was all she talked about whenever they spoke on the telephone. He just didn't have the heart. So, he kept his answers brief and changed the subject at the earliest opportunity. Still, she was so certain that he was heading toward "I do" with the fictional woman he'd named Beth that, finally, he'd just agreed with her.

He wasn't sure where the name had come from. Only that it seemed a suitable moniker for the sensible and sweet woman his grandmother believed had snagged his heart.

His lie had succeeded in easing Nana Jo's mind; now his was in turmoil. She was insisting on meeting his fiancée, and she wouldn't take no for an answer any longer. If Thomas didn't bring the young woman to Nana Jo's home in Charlevoix for the upcoming Fourth of July weekend, she threatened to get in her car and make the long trip downstate to meet his Beth.

He didn't like the idea of his grandmother tooling around town in her vintage Cadillac DeVille, much less getting on an expressway where other vehicles would be whizzing by and no doubt honking their horns in irritation since she always drove at least ten miles per hour below the posted speed limit. But if he told her the truth, she would only go back to insisting that she had one foot in the grave. He couldn't stand the thought of that.

The only solution, as far as he could see, was to produce a fiancée now, and then later, after a reasonable length of time had passed, have that fiancée call things off. If he seemed heartbroken, perhaps Nana Jo would stop pushing so hard, forget about the "dreams" and go back to living her life to the fullest.

A tall order, to be sure. He sighed heavily and closed his eyes.

A tap sounded at his door. "Excuse me, Thomas."

He opened his eyes to find his secretary standing there with a look of concern pinching her features. Annette was two decades older than Thomas and, like his grandmother, she worried about him. She, too, thought he should be married or at least in a serious relationship at this point in his life. As his employee, however, Annette was much less vocal on the subject, thank goodness.

"Is everything all right?" she asked now.

"Headache," he murmured. It wasn't a complete lie. It was Monday and he had until Thursday to figure a way out of this mess. His temples had begun to throb. He pushed back his chair from his desk and started to rise. "I think I'll knock off a little early."

"Oh." Annette's lips pursed.

"Problem?"

"No. Not really. It's just that the head of Literacy Liaisons is here to see you."

"Right now?"

She nodded.

Reaching for his calendar, he said, "I don't recall an appointment being scheduled."

"That's because she doesn't have one. She dropped in unannounced hoping for a few minutes of your time." Annette shook her head. "It's all right. I'll tell her that she needs to make an appointment. Maybe one day next week?"

Thomas held up a hand. "No. That won't be necessary. I'll see her now. Might as well get this over with." He rubbed one temple. "I assume she's after a donation."

His secretary smiled. "I'm sure you're right."

Three things struck Thomas immediately when the young woman entered his office. First, how small she was, despite wearing a pair of three-inch-high pumps that were the same color as her conservative gray pantsuit.

Even in them, he doubted she topped out at five-five.

Second, her mouth. It was wide with full lips that were curving into a smile that lit up a pair of surprisingly dark eyes for one so fair. Add in a slightly upturned, freckle-dusted nose and bobbed blond hair that fell even with a blunt chin, and the adjective *cute* was a far better description for her than beautiful.

Third—and perhaps this was only because he was feeling so desperate—she wasn't wearing a wedding ring. In fact, other than a pair of simple pearl earrings, she wasn't wearing any jewelry at all.

He eyed her speculatively, both ashamed and intrigued by the direction of his thoughts. What if…? Nah.

"Good afternoon, Mr. Waverly. I'm Elizabeth Morris." She extended her right hand. "Thank you for taking the time to see me on such short notice."

He shook her hand. Like the rest of her, it was small. And soft. Her grip, however, was not. It was firm and all business. He liked that about her. There was nothing worse than a limp handshake, even coming from a petite woman who barely looked old enough to order a drink.

"Have a seat," he said.

"I'm pretty sure you've guessed I've come here today to ask for money." Those full lips bowed again, making him appreciate her forthrightness all the more.

The headache he'd been nursing began to disappear. He steepled his fingers in front of him and, in his most businesslike tone, said, "Waverly Enterprises is always interested in helping worthy causes in our community. Why don't you tell me a little bit about yours?"

She exhaled discreetly, as if she hadn't been sure Thomas wouldn't show her the door.

"Literacy Liaisons specializes in helping adults in our community learn to read."

"Is illiteracy really an issue in Ann Arbor?"

She tilted her head to one side. "That surprises you?"

"A little." The city was home to the University of Michigan and one of the best medical facilities in North America.

"Despite the fact that we live in a college town with a lot of highly educated residents, there are people here and in the surrounding communities who are either illiterate or functionally illiterate. That means they may be able to read well enough to get by during, say, a trip to the grocery store, but they cannot read well enough to hold a decent job. Many of them wind up poor, sometimes even homeless."

She inched forward on her chair, warming to her subject. Her face lit with the kind of passion that went hand-in-hand with conviction.

"They aren't intellectually challenged, although many of them do have undiagnosed learning disabilities such as dyslexia. As children, they fell through the cracks in our educational system and now, as adults, they continue to fall through the cracks. Our goal is to change that."

Finished, she shifted back in her seat. Her demeanor remained confident; her expression, determined. The mouse who roared, Thomas thought, more impressed than amused by the description.

"But it takes money," he said.

"It does, even though we rely heavily on volunteers for tutoring, we have to supply materials and, sometimes, day care or even transportation to our offices if the client is indigent. We deal specifically with lower-income people who would not be able to afford such services otherwise."

Intrigued now by the cause as much as by

the woman, he asked, "How long has Literacy Liaisons been in business?"

"Nearly ten years."

"And how long have you worked there?"

"I founded it, Mr. Waverly."

Before he could stop himself, he blurted out, "How old are you?" He apologized immediately. "I'm sorry. It's just that…"

"I look young. I know." She tugged at the lapels of her jacket and added, "My power suit notwithstanding."

Her self-deprecating sense of humor caught him off guard. He'd been sure he'd insulted her with his careless remark. Not sure what else to say—a rarity for him when it came to conversing with a member of the opposite sex—Thomas apologized a second time.

She accepted it with a gracious nod and went on. "I got the idea for Literacy Liaisons while I was in college studying to become a teacher."

"U of M?" he asked. It was his alma mater, which gave them something in common.

But she was shaking her head. "Sorry. I hope it won't have a bearing on your interest in Literacy Liaisons, but I'm a Spartan."

Michigan State? The rivalry between the two Big Ten schools was legendary. He lifted one shoulder. "Good school."

"Good comeback." She laughed. "I take it you're a Wolverine."

"I bleed maize and blue," he admitted, referring to the university's colors.

"Good school," she said, mimicking his earlier reply. They both laughed before she went on. "Long story short, instead of going into a classroom to teach after I earned my certification, I decided to open the center."

Gutsy and not exactly the career path most recent college graduates would have chosen.

"Why?" he asked.

She moistened her lips. "I...saw a need."

There was more to it than that, Thomas thought as he studied her expression. He saw determination there and something else. Sadness?

She was saying, "Our primary funding source has been federal grants and some state Department of Health and Human Services contracts, but money is tight everywhere right now. With tax revenues shrinking at every level of government, cuts have been made. Unfortunately, as vital as having a literate population is to economic prosperity, our funding has been reduced significantly during the past two fiscal years alone."

"So, you're seeking donations from the business community."

"Actually, I'm doing more than that. I want to create an endowment fund to ensure the center's viability both in good economic times and bad. It's not easy to go begging for money, no matter how worthy the cause. I would prefer not to have to do it on an annual basis."

Again, she smiled.

"Then an endowment makes sense."

The more she said, the more impressed he was with her resolve. He couldn't think of another woman in his acquaintance who would have started up a nonprofit right out of college and, a decade later, be pounding the pavement to ensure it remained viable.

Of course, the women he dated tended to be far more egocentric than philanthropic. A good number of them didn't hold a regular job thanks to access to a trust fund or their daddy's continuing indulgence. Physically, they were Elizabeth Morris's polar opposite as well. None had been under five-eight. Indeed, a couple had stood eye-level with him in their bare feet. He favored model types, tall and leggy. Arm candy was what Nana Jo called them. It was an apt description. Every last one of them had been flawlessly beautiful and ultrafashionable. None would be caught dead in Elizabeth Morris's self-described power suit or her nondescript pumps. Which made her somehow all the more perfect.

What if…?

No matter how many times he tried to quell that inappropriate question, it just kept begging to be answered.

She cleared her throat, and he realized he'd been staring. So much for his renowned manners. This made twice in their very short acquaintance that he'd been not only impolite, but also openly rude. Before he could apologize, however, she was rising to her feet.

"I can see that I've taken up enough of your time. I'll just leave you with some additional information about our organization as well as our fundraising campaign. My contact information is in the packet should you have any questions."

There was no hint of a smile on her face as she pulled a folder from her satchel and laid it on his desk. She didn't look angry, but rather disheartened and maybe even a little bit weary. Who could blame her? Thomas imagined she'd probably run into a lot of closed doors and closed wallets during her quest.

"Please. Have a seat. I'll take a look right now," he said, forestalling her departure.

Inside the folder, he wasn't surprised to find several pages of carefully ordered facts about Literacy Liaisons's mission, each one bulleted for easy reading. He'd already determined that she was meticulous and organized. He glanced through the numbers regarding the endowment fund. She was nearly two-thirds of the way to her goal.

Prefacing this, he said, "I see you've been very busy."

"I've been at it for nearly nine months. Unfortunately, it's been slow going lately." She shrugged then and said, "The economy."

Ah, yes. Two words that said it all these days. The economy had wreaked havoc on Waverly Enterprises's bottom line, too, causing Thomas and his department managers to scour the company's budget for savings. The office Christmas party had been scaled back to a luncheon, wages had been frozen and some low-level positions were going unfilled.

Still, he'd tried not to cut back too much on charitable contributions—not because his accountants were quick to remind him that such donations were a tax deduction, but because he genuinely believed in being socially responsible.

Teaching people to read was not just commendable, it was essential. As a businessman, he understood that perfectly. Hers was just the sort of endeavor he preferred to support, especially if the bulk of his donation would go to actual programs rather than overhead, which the paperwork in front of him assured that it would.

The subtle scent of apple blossoms floated his way, and that crazy idea he'd been entertaining since she'd first walked through his door became all the more pronounced.

What if...?

The question no longer seemed so outlandish. Nor did asking it seem totally self-serving. After all, a sizable donation would put her endowment campaign over the top and ensure the future viability of Literacy Liaisons. They could help each other out.

Besides, Elizabeth Morris seemed to be a practical woman, the sort who would see his proposal for what it was: a mutually beneficial business arrangement. *Quid pro quo.*

"So, do you have any questions?" she asked politely. Her smile was back in place and just this side of hopeful.

Did he ever, and it was a doozy, but the one Thomas went with was: "Does anyone ever call you Beth?"

CHAPTER TWO

ELIZABETH felt her mouth fall open. Of all the questions she'd anticipated Thomas Waverly asking, that one wasn't among them. Inquiries about her business or her background? Certainly. Her nickname? Not so much. But since it would be rude to question his questioning— almost as rude as calling on him at his office without an actual appointment—she did her best to wipe away her surprise and answered him honestly.

"No one's ever called me Beth."

Lizzie sometimes, since that had been her actual name. She'd changed it legally once she reached adulthood. She liked the formality of Elizabeth, the utter timelessness of it, not to mention the respect that it seemed to engender. Queens and Hollywood legends were named Elizabeth. Lizzie? Put the word *tin* before it and it referred to a jalopy.

He inhaled deeply, as if preparing to make

an earthshaking announcement. But all he said was, "You look like a Beth."

"Perhaps you have me confused with someone else," she suggested, unsure what else to say.

The conversation had taken an odd and definitely awkward turn, and, even though she hardly could claim to be an expert on men, the speculation brewing in this particular man's gaze was unnerving. Okay, it also was a bit flattering. Men as gorgeous and accomplished as Thomas Waverly rarely gave Elizabeth the time of day—whether or not she'd made an appointment. They certainly didn't look at her like he was looking at her—as if he were interested in something more personal than making a charitable donation.

"Perhaps," he said with a nod before glancing away.

It sounded as if he muttered the word *crazy* half under his breath. If so, the description fit the situation, she decided. More likely, though, she was just imagining things or blowing them out of proportion. It was best to leave before she said something foolish, especially since he seemed interested in her cause.

Elizabeth started to rise. "I'd better be going. Thank you again for your time." She nibbled her bottom lip before adding, "I hope we will be able to count Waverly Enterprises among our contributors."

He pulled her business card from the folder she'd given him and held it up. "I'll be in touch with you. I promise."

"Terrific." She should have been relieved, happy. Why, Elizabeth wondered, did she feel apprehensive? No, what she was feeling wasn't apprehension, but anticipation, an almost foreign sensation where a man was concerned. But then, Thomas Waverly wasn't a man; he was a potential donor with pockets deep enough to push her cause much closer to its goal.

Just as she made that determination, he rose from his seat—a little more than six feet worth of perfectly formed and proportioned male. The custom cut of his suit showcased a pair of broad shoulders and a body made up of lean muscle rather than the kind of soft bulk found on a lot of the desk-bound CEOs she'd called on. Not a man? Those words, unuttered though they'd been, taunted her. Oh, he was a man, all right. And every last inch of him was steeped in testosterone.

The satchel slipped from Elizabeth's hand and landed on the carpeted floor with a thud. Her fingers had gone as slack as her mouth. She snapped her lips closed as he came around his desk. He was bending to retrieve her case even before she managed to move. And here she'd been hoping to make her exit before she could make herself look foolish.

"This thing is pretty heavy." His smile, thank goodness, wasn't awash in amusement.

"Thank you."

Their fingers brushed in the handoff, and she experienced an unprecedented urge to sigh. Oh, it was definitely time to go. During the past month, she had managed to wrest precious little in the way of donations from the local business community, not sizable ones at any rate. Money continued to trickle in—a little here, a little there—but the well of largesse appeared to have run dry. Literacy Liaisons's endowment fund campaign not only needed Waverly Enterprises's support, but it was also desperate for it.

So, without further hesitation, Elizabeth beat a retreat, mentally kicking herself all the way home.

Howie greeted her at the front door of her small bungalow with an enthusiastic kiss after nearly knocking her off her feet. Whether she was gone an hour or all day, her golden retriever-slash-Labrador-slash-a-few-other-kinds-of-canine was always happy to see her.

Ecstatic, in fact. If only every door she

opened held such adoration on the other side, her life and her job would be just that much more enjoyable.

"I missed you, too, boy."

She removed his big paws from her chest and stooped to pick up the scattering of envelopes that had been pushed through the door's mail slot.

Bill, bill, bill, junk, junk and a reminder that one of her magazine subscriptions was about to run out. The internet made communicating with friends, loved ones and business associates quick and easy, but Elizabeth missed receiving actual letters, even if the only person she really hoped to hear from was the one person who would never write. A person who couldn't write. Or read.

Her brother. She hadn't seen him in more than a decade, though he occasionally called their parents. For all intents and purposes, though, Ross had disappeared.

Howie's whining pulled her from the past, reminding her that he needed to go outside and do his business.

When she opened the door, the dog was out in a flash, a bullet of peaches-and-cream-colored fur that pulled up short just before the sidewalk. Elizabeth had installed an electronic fence to keep him within the boundaries of the yard. As she watched him take off after a squirrel in what had become a ritual game of chase, her cell phone rang.

She retrieved it from her satchel. "Hello?"

"Miss Morris?" The deep voice was familiar, but she couldn't quite place it.

"Yes."

"It's Thomas Waverly."

This was a surprise, so much so that the cell phone nearly fell to the floor, much as her bag had in his office. She bobbled it before managing to return it to her ear. The man had a way of making her uncharacteristically clumsy.

"Are you there?" he was asking.

"Yes, sorry. I just wasn't expecting to hear from you." She gave her forehead a slap. "So soon that is."

Cool, collected and confident—that was what she needed to be. Unfortunately, she sounded flustered and slightly breathless—reactions that someone as handsome as Thomas Waverly probably experienced on a regular basis when it came to women.

He was saying, "I was wondering if we could meet to discuss…a donation."

Had she imagined that slight hesitation? Well, no matter. She would clear her calendar if need be to accommodate someone interested in helping her cause. "Certainly. Just name a time and I'll be there."

"I was thinking tonight. Over dinner."

"Dinner. Tonight," she repeated in surprise, and wanted to smack her forehead again.

Put together like that, it sounded as if she thought he was asking her out on a date, which, of course, was ridiculous. Thomas Waverly was a busy man. His time was at a premium. More likely he preferred to get this out of the way so that he didn't have to waste office hours on what, for him at least, amounted to an inconsequential matter. That explanation made sense until a little voice whispered in her head that he needn't be bothered at all. A man of his stature had plenty of subordinates to take care of such things, including the efficient older woman who'd so kindly asked him to see Elizabeth in the first place earlier that day.

As if he could read her mind, Thomas said, "I know it's a little unorthodox, meeting over dinner, but I have something I'd like to discuss with you. An opportunity that is…" He paused again, just long enough to have Elizabeth holding her breath. "Well, in itself, rather unorthodox."

"Oh?" Color her intrigued. Before she could respond further, however, her dog sent up a booming howl of protest as the squirrel he'd been chasing perched on the lowest branch of the front yard's big oak and chattered noisily down at him.

"Howie!" she yelled.

Even though she'd moved the phone away from her mouth, she heard Thomas say, "I apologize. You have company. I should have realized."

Elizabeth nearly laughed out loud at the statement. Did he think she was entertaining a man? More like man's best friend. Sadly, no males of the two-legged variety had darkened her door in several months.

"Not how you mean," she told him, even though she found her dog to be excellent company. She'd rescued Howie from the local pound nearly two years earlier. He'd been on death row, though the pound didn't actually call it that. Still, his fate had been determined, his date with a needle full of sleepy juice scheduled. His crime? Few people wanted a nearly three-year-old, seventy-five-pound pooch who could be every bit as stubborn as he was affectionate. "Howie's my dog. He's chasing a squirrel."

"A futile endeavor, I take it." There was a smile in Thomas's voice.

A fellow dog person? That made him even more appealing in her book.

"Very, which is why he's barking loud enough to wake the dead." She held the phone away from her and covered the mouthpiece long enough to holler the dog's name a second time.

Mrs. Hildabrand, her neighbor from across the street, would be on her front porch any minute to warn Elizabeth that the police would be on the way if Howie didn't quiet down. The elderly woman already had called the authorities twice in the past month with noise complaints. The officers the department sent out had been kind and even understanding. But Elizabeth couldn't afford to press her luck. Thankfully, this time Howie obeyed her command to cease and desist. He trotted to the porch and then through the door she'd opened for him, tail held high and wagging madly, probably for the squirrel's benefit.

"So, about tonight, do you have any plans?" Thomas asked.

"No. Not a thing." Because the stark reply made her sound, well, pathetic, she amended quickly, "What I mean is, nothing that can't be rescheduled."

Or recorded on her DVR. Yes, her social life was that pathetic.

"Terrific."

The relief she heard in his voice left her as curious as what his "unorthodox proposal" might be. After all, Thomas Waverly struck her as the sort of man who was always in control and only asked questions whose answers he already knew. Yet, he was acting very much like he needed her rather than the other way around.

They made arrangements to meet at an Italian restaurant where the highly rated menu came with equally high prices. Elizabeth had eaten at Antonio's exactly once, and then, since she'd gone with a girlfriend, she'd ordered only a bowl of soup. Everything else was beyond her budget, especially once a glass of wine had been factored in.

After hanging up, she paced her living room, absently stopping to pick up the magazines that Howie had knocked off the coffee table with his tail. The dog paced alongside her, his tongue lolling out from his open-mouthed grin.

"I've got an hour before we meet."

Howie panted, as much from his recent exercise as from the heat. The house had no air-conditioning and wouldn't for the foreseeable future. She didn't have the extra funds in her household budget for that kind of luxury. Everything she had, she poured into her work.

"An hour," she repeated. "That's not a lot of time. I need to make the most of it." She let out a laugh that was brittle with nerves. For her benefit as much as the dog's, she added, "I've worked my way through the alphabet when it comes to donors. Obviously, at *W*, I'm getting a little desperate."

Howie stared at her, as if he suspected there was more to those nerves than desperation on behalf of the nonprofit she'd started from scratch a decade before.

"I need to do something to make Thomas Waverly sit up and take notice."

When Elizabeth sat down in front of her laptop, the dog laid his head on her knee. She planned to print out a batch of success stories from Literacy Liaisons's client list. The testimonials were proof of how life-changing learning to read could be. But as she perched on a chair in front of the computer screen, she fiddled with the ends of her hair and became distracted. She was due for a trim.

"Maybe the next time I see my stylist I'll ask about a perm. What do you think, Howie?"

The dog lifted his head from her leg. She

swore he looked confused, and no wonder. Why was she thinking about this now?

"Never mind."

Howie continued to stare at her.

"Look, I know this isn't a date." She patted his broad head. Again, for his benefit as well as her own, she said, "But it never hurts to look one's best. Dress for success and all that."

With that in mind, she snatched up the phone and dialed her best friend's number, sighing with relief when Melissa Sutton picked up just before the call would have gone to voice mail. It was hard to catch her very social friend, even on her cell.

The two women had been tight since college, even though they seemed to have little in common with the exception of their commitment to battling illiteracy, which was why after a stint as a packaging engineer, Melissa had showed up at Literacy Liaisons, willing to take a significant cut in pay for rewards of another kind.

The similarities ended there. Where Elizabeth was reserved and, admittedly, a bit of a wallflower, her friend, who was nearly as petite as Elizabeth, managed to stand out. It wasn't only her infectious laughter and bawdy sense of humor that caught men's attention.

Mel was a bona fide head-turner. On more than one occasion, Elizabeth had witnessed her friend's effect on men. It was almost comical the way they fawned over her and catered to her every whim. If only that kind of charisma could be bottled up and sold.

"I have an emergency," she said in a rush.

"My God, Elizabeth, what's wrong?"

"I need some of your clothes."

"My clothes?"

"I have an important meeting in roughly an hour and nothing suitable to wear."

"You're having a fashion emergency?" Mel's laughter boomed. "I think I need to sit down."

"It's not funny."

"Sorry." Her friend's tone turned serious. "It's just I've never had you call to borrow clothes for a date let alone for work."

"This is important."

"So you've already said. Work shouldn't be more important than your love life. That's just sad, honey. Sad." Elizabeth thought she heard a *tsking* sound before Mel went on. "You need to get out more, kick up your heels. And the heels I'm referring to are not those dowdy pair of black pumps that would suit my great-aunt Geraldine."

Elizabeth pinched her eyes closed. "Can we have this conversation another time, please?"

"Fine. Another time. And don't think I won't hold you to it," Mel warned, then added, "So, am I coming to your place or are you coming to mine?"

They decided on Mel's since her two-story town house was closer to the restaurant Thomas had selected, and it wouldn't require her friend to pack up an assortment of outfits.

Once there, Mel wasn't satisfied with dressing Elizabeth in a ruffled shift that was surprisingly flattering on her less curvaceous form, and pairing the soft pink number with strappy silver sandals. She insisted on restyling her hair and applying additional makeup, too.

The effect was an improvement, and she hardly appeared overmade, but it still presented Elizabeth with a dilemma.

Studying her reflection in Mel's vanity mirror, she said, "He's going to think I'm interested in him."

"He who?" Mel asked, leaning over to dab a little more coral-colored gloss on Elizabeth's bottom lip.

"Thomas Waverly."

Her friend drew back, eyes wide with surprise. "Thomas Waverly? *GQ*-cover-worthy

Thomas Waverly? That's who you're having dinner with?"

"Do you know him?" Her stomach pitched. Had Mel dated him? That question was followed rapidly by: Why would that matter?

"I know *of* him," Mel clarified. "I saw him at a celebrity golf outing that I played with Dominic last summer."

Dominic, right. Mel's beau of the month several months ago. A corporate highflyer of some sort. Yet for all the money he'd lavished on Mel, he'd been downright stingy when it came to contributing to Literacy Liaisons.

"So, what's Thomas like?"

"We didn't actually meet, but I saw him tee off on one of the par threes. Very nice swing. Fluid and strong. He nearly wound up with a hole in one. He settled for a birdie thanks to one very smooth putting stroke." Mel made a purring sound that kick-started Elizabeth's barely settled nerves.

"Do you ever *not* think of sex?"

Mel propped one hip on the edge of the bathroom counter. "I only think of it so often to take up the slack for you. You need to think of it more."

"I don't have the time." A pitiful excuse, and, of course, Mel called her on it.

"Yes, it would be a real shame to miss your

evening line-up of cable television shows once in a while."

"You like to watch *White Collar*, too."

"I like to watch the hunky guy who plays the ex-con," Mel clarified while examining her manicure. "But I'm not faithful to him. When I have a better offer, I go out."

Elizabeth scowled. "I haven't had any better offers." Indeed, she hadn't had any offers in months.

"Because you make sure every guy around thinks you're only interested in your work," her friend said.

"It's important."

"That goes without saying, Elizabeth. And I understand why it's so important to you. But—"

She put a hand out, pushing away the pain even as she redirected the conversation. "Can we get back to the crisis at hand, please?"

Mel sighed heavily. "Fine, but just so you know, I don't see Thomas Waverly as a crisis. In fact, I find myself a little jealous of you. He's one very prime specimen."

"I hadn't noticed." Elizabeth managed a nonchalant tone.

Mel wasn't fooled. In fact, she nearly doubled over with laughter. Her mirth echoed off the bathroom tiles.

"Oh, please. You'd have to be dead not to notice, and even then I have a feeling that man could raise a woman's pulse rate. Are you really going to sit there and tell me you don't find him hot?"

"He's attractive," Elizabeth allowed.

Mel merely raised her brows at the bland assessment.

"Okay. He's gorgeous. Drop-dead so. But we're not going out on a date, Mel." Elizabeth glanced at her reflection again. She liked what she saw—the softer hairstyle, the somewhat smoky eyes, the flirty dress. But that was the problem. She looked like a woman who was ready for an evening out. "I don't want him to think that I think it's a date."

Mel pursed her lips. Unlike Elizabeth's, they were an inviting pink color without any added gloss. "Why would that be a problem?"

"This is business. I need his donation."

"I understand that, but I don't think that's the real answer."

Elizabeth sighed. "You know me too well."

"And don't forget it. So, answer the question." She crossed her arms in challenge.

"Come on. Look at me, Mel."

"I am looking. I see a beautiful woman, not to mention one who is exceedingly smart and interesting."

Elizabeth rolled her eyes. "Well, I am wearing your clothes."

"I'm not just talking about what you've got on or the way your hair is styled, though that little finger-fluffing trick is flattering and a little extra gloss does wonders for what is already a great set of lips. But clothes, a different hairdo and a little more makeup don't make you smart and interesting. That's all you, honey." She waited a beat before adding, "That dress does make you sexy, though."

Mel's perfectly arched brows bobbed twice for emphasis.

Her friend's words should have done wonders for Elizabeth's ego, but Elizabeth had never had much confidence in her looks. She chalked that up to the fact that from an early age her post-hippie parents had discouraged any sort of "enhancement" or improvement to one's appearance. Both her folks sported long hair. Her mother wore hers in an unflattering ponytail. Her father's was twisted into dreadlocks that streamed halfway to his waist. Skeet Morris didn't believe in shaving. Neither did Elizabeth's mother, Delphine. *Anywhere*. To this day her parents were mortified that Elizabeth wore her hair short and styled, dressed in conservative garb and had plucked the unibrow she'd sported throughout high school into two distinct arches.

"You're my friend," she reminded Mel.

"That doesn't mean I can't be objective. Your problem, Elizabeth, is that you've spent your entire life blending into the background, so it makes you uncomfortable when you stand out."

"That's not true." Not completely anyway. She was perfectly happy to stand out when it came to her job.

Mel crossed her arms over her chest again. "It's a fact."

"Okay, we're getting off track here. I'm not after the man. I'm after his money." When her friend's lips twitched, she added, "You know what I mean. This is about a donation to Literacy Liaisons, one that very well could be large enough that you and I can sit back and relax for a while…figuratively speaking."

But Mel wasn't buying it. "I've never understood the big deal with mixing business with pleasure. As long as both parties go into it with their eyes wide open, why not? You're both adults."

Nerves fluttered in Elizabeth's belly. "Maybe I should send you to meet with him. You're a lot better at this sort of thing than I am."

Mel manufactured an insulted expression and said, "Excuse me?"

"You know what I mean. Men swarm to you. Thomas Waverly would be putty in your hands. In fact, maybe I should have been sending you to call on potential donors all along. We'd already have our endowment."

"Oh, no. No thanks." Mel was shaking her head. "I'm good at flirting, honey, not finalizing deals. Besides, I prefer to remain behind the scenes."

"So you always say." Elizabeth reached for a tissue and blotted off a little of the coral-colored gloss. "I just don't want to give Mr. Waverly the impression that I would be willing to sleep with him in order to ensure that he cuts the agency a sizable check."

Mel winked. "Does that mean you'd be willing to sleep with him for reasons more primal?"

"God, Mel!" Elizabeth's nerves kicked up again.

"Just askin'." Grinning, her friend pointed to her wristwatch. "You'd better get going, Cinderella. Your ball is about to begin."

CHAPTER THREE

THOMAS did a double take when Elizabeth walked through the door of Antonio's. He'd arrived at the restaurant a few minutes early, assuming that he would have plenty of time to gather his thoughts and plot out his pitch. All of the women he knew were notorious for being late, in part because they preferred to make grand entrances. He should have known Elizabeth would be different. That was, after all, part of her appeal for the role he was about to ask her to play.

Even arriving early, she managed to make an entrance. No mouths dropped opened in awe, and conversations continued as before. But something inside of Thomas shifted before going oddly still. He couldn't take his eyes off of her.

Who knew cute also could be so sexy?

Since their meeting a few hours earlier, she'd changed her clothes. No real surprise, since he had as well, trading in his business attire for a more casual pair of pants and a button-down shirt. He'd left off his tie, too, but he found himself tugging at his collar anyway.

Her transformation was far more dramatic. He wouldn't have expected the woman he'd met in the severely cut suit and serviceable pumps to own such a fashionable outfit and shoes. The lines of the dress and the heels gave her the illusion of greater height. As small as she was, she had a pair of killer legs.

Because he felt himself beginning to ogle them, he returned his gaze to her face. That wasn't the safer bet, he realized immediately. She'd done something different with her hair. It was no longer quite so straight and tidy. *Tousled* was the word that came to mind. He wondered if it would feel as soft as it appeared. As for that mobile mouth of hers, it was now twice as inviting thanks to a slick coat of tinted gloss. How would it taste?

Uh-oh.

He scrambled to put the brakes on the hormones that threatened to rev into hyperdrive. Given what he was about to propose, quite literally, he couldn't afford to let anything more than business transpire between them. He couldn't have her thinking he wanted more

than what he was offering: a mutually beneficial business arrangement.

He stood when she reached the table. It was
second nature, thanks to his grandmother,
as was pulling out Elizabeth's chair. In fact,
Thomas beat the maitre d' to it. The man
smiled uncomfortably before withdrawing.

"Sorry I'm late," she said, as she settled in
her seat.

Thomas glanced at his watch, even though
it wasn't necessary. "Actually, you're early."

"But not as early as you are."

He shrugged and sat down. "It's a habit of
mine."

A bad one according to the last four women
he'd dated, those grand entrances and all.
They didn't appreciate answering the doorbell
before they were ready to wow him with what
waited on the other side.

"A good one," Elizabeth said, as if reading
his mind. "There's nothing worse than keeping people waiting, at least in my book."

Thomas agreed wholeheartedly, but that
didn't change his plan to keep her waiting,
at least until the entrée course, before he
started his pitch. By that point, he was hoping
she wouldn't stand up and walk out on him,
though he wasn't ruling out the possibility.

He bided his time, relying on small talk as

their drinks arrived. She went with a glass of plain water garnished with a wedge of lemon. Although he wanted to brace himself with a scotch, neat, he settled for red wine, which he intended to sip slowly. He needed to keep a clear head—especially since the woman seated opposite him was having a definite, if odd, effect on his equilibrium. Nerves, he told himself. After all, he had a lot riding on the outcome of the evening. But then, so did she.

By the time the waiter brought their salads and a basket of warm rolls, they had thoroughly dissected the extended weather forecast for the upcoming holiday weekend. It was amazing how much people could talk without really saying anything. Recalling the passion and conviction with which Elizabeth had described her agency's mission to him earlier, he had a feeling she would be an engaging conversationalist if they ever strayed from the standard polite topics. Because he wanted to, he didn't. Stay with the script. This wasn't a date.

Finally, their dinners arrived and the moment of truth was at hand. She'd just taken the first bite of her grilled salmon when he put down his fork and cleared his throat. She glanced over in question. Now or never, he decided.

"I mentioned on the phone that I had an unusual proposal for you."

She nodded, swallowed. "*Unorthodox* is how I believe you phrased it."

"Yes. It is. Very." He swallowed as well, even though he had not yet touched his steak or the sautéed baby portabella mushrooms in wine sauce that smothered it. "I want to assure you, this isn't something I make a habit of."

Thomas had hoped to sound reassuring, but her expression made it clear he was doing a lousy job of it. She appeared a little alarmed, and no wonder given the way he was acting. Better just to get right to it, he decided, except that he didn't. Rather, he went on in uncharacteristic bumbling fashion.

"It's just that I find myself in a tight spot. I told someone—someone very dear to me—that I am…that is, that I have been seeing…" He laughed uncomfortably. "This is awkward."

Across from him, Elizabeth smiled encouragingly, though he thought he saw her glance toward the exit.

"The long and the short of it is I need…I need a…" His gaze focused in on her mouth and he swore his own started to water. "I need a woman."

Elizabeth wasn't sure whether to be flattered that he'd singled her out or concerned for her safety given his intense stare. One thing she knew for certain, she was curious. Why on earth did he need a woman? Surely female companionship was not in short supply for a man as successful and handsome as he was. There had to be a rational explanation for what he'd just said.

So, in her most polished business tone, she inquired politely, "Exactly what do you need a woman for, Mr. Waverly?"

"To act as my fiancée."

He was exhaling in a gust, even as Elizabeth's breathing stopped. She hadn't seen this coming.

"Are you asking…? You want me to…? You want to get married?" Her voice rose on the last word. Some of the restaurant's other patrons glanced their way.

"No. Actually, I just need someone to pose as my fiancée for a while." He smiled weakly. "So, um, under the circumstances, I think you should call me Thomas."

She rubbed her right temple in lieu of a response. She'd fallen into an alternative universe. That was the only explanation that made sense. She was wearing Mel's dress and had somehow become, well, Mel. Except that in the big mirror on the wall behind Thomas, she could see her reflection. The dress was Mel's, but Elizabeth was definitely the woman wearing it. And looking gobsmacked. She snapped her mouth closed.

"I know. Crazy, right?" Thomas said on an uncomfortable laugh.

"Certifiable," she agreed.

Both of them were, because, Elizabeth now knew for sure that she was feeling flattered. Thomas Waverly, successful businessman and five-alarm hottie, wanted *her* to act as his fiancée? But…

"Why?" she managed to ask at last.

His expression sobered. "Before we get to that, I want to make it clear that I'm not expecting you to do me a favor. I was thinking more like, we could, uh, do each other a favor. You help me out by posing as my intended, and I personally match the donation I've already decided to make to Literacy Liaisons on Waverly Enterprises's behalf. Between those two contributions, your endowment will be realized."

Because her mouth threatened to fall open again, she took a sip of her water. This was more than she'd hoped for. It was everything she wanted, being handed to her on a silver platter. A silver platter held by one of the most eligible bachelors in the city. She checked the mirror a second time, giving that alternative universe theory another go. The same baffled-looking blonde as before gaped back at her. Again, Elizabeth asked, "Why?"

"Right." He reached for his wine and took a sip. Setting the glass back on the table, he said, "Here's the thing. I told my grandmother that I was involved in a serious relationship with a woman."

"Serious as in headed toward the altar."

"Right. The problem is I'm not, but she's expecting to meet, um, my significant other…" He coughed. Choked? Before spitting out, "This weekend."

The long holiday weekend was mere days away, and Elizabeth already had made plans to spend part of it with her parents at their annual soy burger-and-tofu barbecue, but that wasn't what bothered her. Flattery only went so far. As did business dealings.

Her tone took on an edge that she rarely used and had never allowed to seep into her professional life when she said, "You lied to your grandmother?"

Hot or not, the man dropped several points in her estimation. Make that numerous points, and still counting. She didn't care how hand-some he was or how successful. Nor did it matter how desperate she was for his dual donation—and, *God*, she was desperate for that donation. But a man who would lie to a frail, helpless little old lady—and that was the image that came to Elizabeth's mind—was a jerk. End of story. She retrieved the napkin from her lap and set it on the table, fully intending to leave.

Thomas rose part way from his chair as she stood. "Please. Stay and hear me out."

"You lied to your grandmother," she repeated flatly.

"Yes. I did. It sounds horrible, I know." He dropped back into his seat.

"That's one word for it," Elizabeth replied crisply, unwilling to let him off the hook, no matter how appealing he looked wriggling from it. Still, he did look remorseful. Slowly, she returned to her seat and spread the napkin back over her lap. What would it hurt to hear him out?

"Let me give you a little background before you form a solid opinion of the situation." Thomas held out his hands in appeal. "She claimed to be dying and, well, seeing me happily settled is a priority for her. I was hoping to take her mind off her aches and pains."

"Your grandmother is dying?"

"Her doctor says no, but…" His shoulders

lifted in a shrug. "She's sure she is. And she's not easily dissuaded once her mind is made up. I hate seeing her so troubled, especially when there's no need to be. I'm fine. Perfectly happy, in fact. I'm just not married and making great-grandbabies for her to spoil."

"So you're lying to her to protect her?"

"I don't want to lie at all, but yes. If she thinks I'm heading toward 'I do,' then she'll be able to enjoy her life again. She deserves that."

"That's…sweet." And it was.

At least his unorthodox offer was rooted in something other than blatant self-interest. Still, what he was suggesting was crazy, but no more so than the fact that Elizabeth was actually considering it.

"Do you really think your grandmother would buy that you and I are…" She made a winding motion with her index finger, unable to speak the actual words. "I can't believe I'm your usual type."

She wasn't angling for a compliment. She wasn't expecting him to tell her that she was beautiful or even that he found her attractive. Expecting? No. But part of her must have been hoping, she realized, when her heart pinched painfully at his reply.

"You're not my type in the least, which, in

a way, makes you perfect. My grandmother knows the sort of women I prefer to date. Since I've never allowed something serious to begin with them, she assumes that's because I've been dating women who are all wrong for me."

"Have you been?" She immediately shook her head. "I'm sorry. That's really none of my business." Even if she was, at this very moment, considering becoming his bride-to-be, at least for appearances' sake.

"Possibly. Probably." He shrugged carelessly. "I'm not looking for a deep and committed relationship. That's not what I'm after."

Ah, one of those. Elizabeth had dated a couple such men just out of college, not that she'd known their preferences going in, of course. Nope. She'd found out the hard way and wound up with a dinged-up heart for her naiveté.

"Which reminds me," Thomas was saying. "I never thought to ask if you were seeing someone."

His complexion bleached a little as he awaited her reply. She wasn't trying to exploit that with her hesitation. She just wanted to find a way to relay her single status without making herself sound like a loser.

"I date here and there," she said at last. "But I'm not seeing anyone in particular."

"Terrific." He had the grace to grimace. "That came out wrong. What I mean is if you agreed to act as my fiancée, I wouldn't want to put you in an awkward position."

She appreciated that, but... "Excuse me for saying so, Mr....er...Thomas. The situation is already awkward. I barely know you. We met only today. And you're asking me to pose as your fiancée in an attempt to fool your elderly grandmother into believing you've found your soul mate."

He grimaced again. "It sounds even worse when you say it. In my defense, there's nothing for me to gain here. I'm doing this for the right reasons, even if I seem to be going about it the wrong way. I love my grandmother, Elizabeth. She's pretty much all the family I have. She basically raised me."

So many layers to the man, Elizabeth thought. She wanted him to be what he first appeared when he suggested the arrangement: shallow and callous. Then it would be much easier to tell him no, the sizable donations he was promising be damned. She had standards. She had principles. She also apparently had a soft spot for men who had soft spots for their aging grandmothers.

"Why don't you tell me a little bit about her," she suggested, folding her hands in her lap.

"Nana Jo?"

Nana Jo. Cute. He scored another point in his favor. Elizabeth smiled her encouragement.

"She's a pistol." His expression turned fond. "She has an opinion on everything and offers it freely, whether you want to hear it or not."

"My mother's that way, too." Elizabeth had little doubt her expression was one hundred and eighty degrees from fond. She shook off all thoughts of Delphine. "And right now Nana Jo's opinion is that you should be married."

"Actually, that's been her opinion since I graduated from college." He shrugged.

"But you're not marriage-minded. Commitment's not your thing. You prefer to keep your options open and continue to play the field." She paraphrased his earlier comment.

His frown came as a surprise. She got the feeling he wasn't happy with her assessment, though he didn't try to correct her.

"About a year ago, my grandmother started telling me she didn't have long for this life and that the only way she could leave this world peacefully was to know I was settled and happy."

"That's because she loves you."

"And I love her. I'd do anything for her. As I said, she raised me."

Elizabeth tamped down the questions begging to be asked. Chief among them: Where were his parents when he was growing up? Was he, like Mel, the product of a broken home? She pitied him if that were true. Skeet and Delphine might not believe in the institution of marriage, so their exchange of vows was unrecognized by the state as legally binding, but they were committed to one another in their own way. As counterculture and plain old wacky as they could be, at least Elizabeth had the luxury of an intact family. Or she had until her brother decided to drop out of high school and then drop out of sight.

Thomas was saying, "I told her I was seeing someone special mostly to give her something positive to occupy her thoughts. It worked a little too well and spiraled out of control. From that simple statement she extrapolated my impending nuptials."

"And you didn't do anything to stop her?"

"I didn't have the heart. It made her so happy. She went from telling me which outfit she wanted to be buried in to what she planned to wear to my wedding. A pink organdy gown, by the way. She sent me a magazine clipping of it, as well as suggestions for my tuxedo. Black tails. Very formal and timeless, in her opinion."

One corner of his mouth lifted in a bemused smile that tugged at Elizabeth's heart. Oh, he'd dug himself a deep hole all right.

"Why not tell her the truth now? They say honesty is the best policy for a reason."

"I've thought about it. Believe me. But I'm afraid Nana Jo will just go back to fretting over her health and my future, and dropping brochures for headstones in the mail to me."

"But you actually don't plan to get married to me or anyone," she pointed out. "Eventually, your grandmother is going to figure that out."

"I know." He rubbed his chin. "Which is why I was thinking that, after a reasonable length of time, I would tell her that things between you and I had ended."

"My doing, of course."

He smiled guiltily. "She'd be upset. But I think she also would be a little relieved that I almost made it to the altar."

"Commitment phobia cured?"

With one eye closed, he squinted at her with the other. "You don't pull any punches," he said wryly. "I had you pegged as practical, but not quite so blunt."

"That's my professional persona," she reminded him. "I can hardly afford to insult someone who is about to cut my agency a check."

"Present company excluded, of course."

"Your check—"

"Checks. One from my business. One from me."

"Whether one check or two, they are coming with a lot of strings," she reminded him.

"I want to make one thing clear. The check from Waverly Enterprises will be forthcoming regardless. I believe in your cause, and I respect what you're doing."

Slightly mollified, she said, "Thank you."

"As for the other check, the one from me personally, yes, it does have strings as you called them. But I prefer to think of them as conditions, in which case they would serve to keep what would go on between us a business transaction as well, just with the funds coming from my personal bank account rather than my company's."

That made some sense, but… "I'm not saying I agree, but let's discuss that business transaction. What exactly would it entail?"

"Some of your time, for starters. We would need to get up to speed on each other in short order. We're supposed to have been dating for several months. Beyond knowing that you have a dog named Howie and started your nonprofit just after college graduation, I don't know anything about you."

"I could write up some notes."

"Crib sheets, you mean?" His smile was engaging.

"I never had to resort to them myself." She regretted the chiding comment when his lips flattened into a thin line.

"For the record, I'm not a fan of cheating, or lying, although I can understand where you might find that hard to believe right now. See, this is exactly the reason we need to spend time together before this weekend."

"Assuming I agree."

"Assuming that. Yes."

"So, I would meet your grandmother and visit with her over the weekend?"

"That's right. She's incredibly easy to talk to and fun to be around. She plays a mean game of cribbage. Who knows, you might even enjoy yourself," he said.

"Assuming I agree to do this," she repeated.

"Assuming."

But they both seemed to know she was leaning in that direction.

"I won't lie to her, Thomas." This time, his given name slipped easily from Elizabeth's lips. It was important they were clear on this point. She might be willing to bend her principles, but she would not break them. "For her to assume is one thing, but if she flat-out asks me a question that requires me to lie, I won't do it."

"This is assuming you agree." He beat her to it this time.

"Let me make something else clear. The only reason I am even entertaining the possibility of doing this is because Literacy Liaisons means so much to me."

"I know that."

Of course he did. He was banking on it, she realized.

"So, is that a yes?"

She exhaled slowly, knowing her life was about to take a huge and unexpected turn. "Yes."

Once Elizabeth agreed, the rest of dinner passed in a blur for Thomas. When it came time for the check, he didn't remember eating, possibly because more than half of his steak remained untouched on his plate, as did the side of risotto and steamed vegetables.

He was relieved that she'd said yes, of course. Her agreement was what he'd hoped for. Still, he couldn't quite shake his apprehension. Now, he had a fiancée—a woman who was also a stranger. He needed to remedy their unfamiliarity and fast.

As he walked her to her car a little later, he said, "So, I'll see you tomorrow."

She stopped, blinked. "Tomorrow?"

"We only have a few days to get to know one another as well as two people who have been dating for several months would," he reminded her.

"Oh, is that all?" He appreciated her attempt at humor, even if her smile was forced. "So, where and what time?"

"Does nine o'clock work for you?"

Her brow crinkled. "It's a little late," she began. "I'm an early riser, which means I tend to turn in not long after the sun sets."

"In the morning," he clarified.

"Oh. Well, I have to work."

"Yes. I realize that. I was hoping maybe I could come by your offices, see what you do. You can tell anyone who asks that I'm a potential contributor, which is true," he added, in case she was going to remind him that she wasn't willing to lie outright about their relationship.

"Hmm." He watched as Elizabeth mentally flipped through her morning's schedule. "I think that will work."

"Terrific."

Their plans for the next day finalized, they stood in awkward silence beside her car. Though this wasn't an actual date, it had all the hallmarks of a first one thanks to the potent combination of anticipation and apprehension he was feeling. Thomas stuffed his hands into his front pockets and rocked back on his heels.

"So…"

"Thanks for dinner."

Since she'd already thanked him twice on the short walk to her car, he said, "You're welcome. Again."

"Well…" She held up her keys and gave them a shake.

This wouldn't do. Not in the least. Nana Jo was too canny to believe that he and Elizabeth were wildly attracted to one another, much less mildly smitten, given their stilted behavior. Thomas might not want to be in love, but he knew how people in love acted.

Before she could slide onto the driver's seat, he stopped her by saying, "I think we need to get something out of the way right now."

"What?"

"This."

He pulled his hands from his pockets, framed her face with them and leaned down, unable to resist the sweet temptation of those full lips. He thought he heard her sigh. He knew he wanted to moan, and that was before her lips parted. His hands moved from her face to her shoulders and then down to her waist, pulling her closer. It was the small hands lightly touching his back that unnerved him.

He didn't trust himself with her, he realized. He didn't trust himself not to become greedy and demanding. He drew back—but not too quickly; trust be damned, he wanted to savor her—and gazed into a pair of surprised dark eyes.

It must have been his libido-fueled imagination talking, but he swore she asked, "Why did you stop?"

"I…I…"

While he stammered, she took a step back, creating an acceptable amount of space between their bodies. This time, he heard her clearly when she said, "Why did you do that?"

"Sorry." The apology was second nature. It slipped out even before he could wonder if he meant it. She accepted it with a nod, but appeared to be waiting for an explanation. Did he have one?

He knew what his reason for the kiss had been before their mouths met: to put them both at ease about any upcoming shows of affection intended for his grandmother's benefit. And, okay, he'd been a little curious, too. What man wouldn't be when looking at that pair of perfect lips? But how to explain the latter to Elizabeth without damning himself, especially since he'd made it clear their supposed relationship was for show only? So, he went with the former. Sort of.

"I thought it might take the edge off."

Her eyebrows shot up, and no wonder. As explanations went, this one had a decidedly sexual overtone. It also was inaccurate, as he knew only too well. That kiss hadn't taken the edge off of anything. Not in the least. If anything, it had heightened his curiosity. What other secrets were hidden beneath the woman's prim exterior?

He tried again and said, "It's just that people who are engaged and presumably in love are expected to kiss and be affectionate with one another."

Hell, most people assumed engaged couples were doing a whole lot more than that. Just that fast, the image of he and Elizabeth embroiled in a heated encounter flashed through his brain. Scorched through it, more like. It was all he could do to keep a moan from escaping.

"I guess you're right," Elizabeth said. She looked about as off balance as he felt.

"My grandmother will expect to see us touch one another and be comfortable doing so."

He reached over and tucked some hair behind one of her ears, testing himself. It was every bit as soft as he'd assumed it would be.

"Okay." He watched her swallow.

"So, tomorrow. Around nine."

"At my office." She smiled uncertainly, probably wondering what she'd gotten herself into, he thought.

"At your office."

"See you then."

"Looking forward to it." A polite response that was also disturbingly honest in this case.

She slipped behind the wheel of her car. Thomas closed the door and stepped back, offering a wave once she started the engine and shifted into Drive.

Long after he lost sight of her taillights in the flow of traffic, he stood in the parking lot of Antonio's. He was going to have no problem convincing Nana Jo that he found Elizabeth Morris attractive. No problem at all. Which caused him to wonder: What had he just gotten himself into?

CHAPTER FOUR

"So, HOW did it go last night?" Mel asked the next morning as she and Elizabeth sat at the small round table tucked into the corner of Elizabeth's office at Literacy Liaisons. Her friend grinned broadly. "Did you seal the deal and get great gobs of money for our endowment fund?"

"Not exactly," Elizabeth hedged.

She sipped her coffee, her fourth cup so far, and tried to think of a less damning way to explain the "deal" that Thomas had proposed. She still couldn't quite wrap her mind around what he'd suggested...er...proposed. Much less the fact that she had agreed. She told herself it was the agency's needs that caused her to tell him she'd do it, but every time she recalled that kiss in the parking lot, she knew she was lying.

She replayed it now, remembering the feel of Thomas's mouth when it met hers. He'd watched her carefully—curiously?—not closing his eyes until the last moment. Elizabeth knew this because she'd kept both of hers wide open, afraid even to blink lest she find him and the entire evening a figment of her imagination.

But a figment didn't kiss like he did. No one she'd ever met had kissed like he did, evoking responses and tugging forward needs she didn't know she possessed. Thomas had ended the contact before things could progress too far. She'd wanted to think that he was being considerate, chivalrous even. The man was so courteous. His expression, however, said otherwise. He looked surprised, a reaction that could be taken a couple different ways, unfortunately, one of them not so flattering.

"Earth to Elizabeth. Earth to Elizabeth." Mel was snapping her fingers. Then she demanded, "What exactly does 'not exactly' mean?"

"Well, what it means is…um, it means—"

"That I haven't presented her with the check yet."

Thomas stood in the doorway, his expression infused with amusement and something else Elizabeth couldn't quite decipher. Was he embarrassed? Uncertain? Was he recalling that kiss that he'd said had been intended to put both of them at ease? And—God!—what if it actually *had* put him at ease?

"Mr. Waverly!" She shot to her feet. Her hip bumped the table's edge and her coffee spilled, spreading over the tabletop in a brown wave and threatening to drip into Mel's lap.

"I thought we agreed you would call me Thomas." His smile was engaging and just this side of intimate, no doubt for Mel's benefit. Before either woman could react, he walked over, took the handkerchief from his pocket and laid it over the puddle of java to prevent further damage.

Not that the coffee was what held Elizabeth's attention. No. It was the man and the ridiculous effect he was having on her. One simple smile—calculated for maximum impact, most likely, since everything between them was intended for show—and her insides were whipping around like the blades of a ceiling fan stuck on high. But who could blame her? Look at him. He was gorgeous. The lean cheeks and square jaw. The blue-green eyes set off by slashing dark brows. The tidy hair that was just this side of black. And that build. She couldn't help it. She sighed.

No matter what he wore, he wore it well. Already, she'd seen him in casual attire and a three-piece suit. Today, he'd paired a herring-bone jacket with dark jeans, managing to look more put-together and sophisticated than men who were going for just that effect.

Meanwhile, she was back to wearing sack-cloth. Well, not exactly. But she might as well have been. Her stint as Cinderella had ended, and Mel's borrowed clothes had been returned. In their place, Elizabeth had tucked a plain white blouse into a navy pencil skirt. The strand of imitation pearls around her neck added little in the way of embellishment to an otherwise boring outfit.

The sad thing was she'd picked it out with care that morning, hoping for simple sophisti-cation. Now, she merely felt plain, especially sitting next to Mel, who wore a leopard-print wrap dress tamed by a black blazer.

"I wasn't expecting you yet. You're early," Elizabeth said. She glanced at her wrist before realizing no watch was strapped to it. She'd opted to leave it off today since it was a little clunky.

Mel cleared her throat, reminding Elizabeth of her manners.

"Oh. Mr.….Thomas." She managed a smile. "This is my good friend Melissa Sutton. Mel's in charge of Literacy Liaisons's volunteers, both recruiting them and then training them to tutor our clients."

Elizabeth held her breath after the introduction, well aware of the effect her best friend had on men. Not that it mattered in this instance. From a purely practical standpoint, however, it wouldn't do for him to be attracted to other women if he was trying to convince his grandmother he'd fallen head over heels for Elizabeth.

He smiled politely and pumped Mel's hand. A cadre of bangle bracelets jangled. Thomas, however, showed no outward sign of being interested.

Hmm. This was a first. Elizabeth had witnessed men of all ages—married, single and every status in between—come on to Mel in one form or another with no encouragement whatsoever. A young seminary student had opted not to pursue the priesthood after meeting her, such was her friend's natural allure. But Thomas's only interest in Mel apparently was to point out, "My handkerchief didn't cover everything, I'm afraid. You'll be wearing some of that coffee if you don't move."

"Oh!" Mel glanced down and managed to shift out of harm's way a second before coffee dribbled over the table's edge. She divided her gaze between Thomas and Elizabeth as she rose. "I'll just go get something to clean this with."

"It was nice meeting you," Thomas said.

"The same." Mel offered a cheerful smile. She waited till she was at the door and Thomas's back was to her before she mouthed to Elizabeth, "Oh, my God!"

"I hope I didn't catch you at a bad time," Thomas said. "I did say nine."

The clock on the wall read eight forty-five. He was early again, which she should have expected. But Elizabeth had been running uncharacteristically late all morning. She hadn't slept well. In fact, other than a couple of hours just before her alarm went off, she hadn't slept at all. Who could blame her? Forget Thomas's "proposal," it was that kiss that had caused her insomnia.

She touched her lips now, remembering it, savoring it. Lost in recalling exactly how his mouth had felt pressed to hers, it took her a moment to realize that the man responsible for that kiss was smiling at her. She pulled her fingers away.

"Nine. Right. You said nine." She nodded, mortified at the way she was acting. "I remember that now."

He nodded, too. Then, when the silence

threatened to become awkward, he spread his hands wide. "So, this is Literacy Liaisons."

Work. Good. Excellent. It was the center of her life, what she poured most of her time and effort into, which meant it would be easy to talk about. And that would help take her mind off how sexy Thomas looked in that herringbone blazer and crisp blue oxford shirt sans necktie.

"Let me show you around," she suggested.

She started in the main meeting room, which resembled a classroom, with the letters of the alphabet posted on the walls along with pictures that corresponded to the sounds those letters made. Instead of rows of desks, however, there was a large conference table. Elizabeth had found that adults responded better to that setting than the more traditional one. Some of them had had bad experiences with school. Others were embarrassed by their situation. A conference table made it seem more like a workplace. Even though they were students in the true sense of the word, her clients also felt more like respected adults here. She explained that to Thomas.

He glanced around, nodding in appreciation. "I guess I never thought of it that way."

"It's not an issue for some people, but when we realized it was for a lot of our clients…"

She shrugged. "The goal is to make them as comfortable as possible so they can focus all of their attention on learning to read."

"How exactly do you do that? The teaching, I mean."

"There are a variety of different methods. For instance, the Barton Reading and Spelling System has proved a good fit for a number of our clients. It focuses on phonics and recognizing the sounds letters make."

Thomas's nod was perfunctory. He found her work interesting, but the woman even more so. His gaze kept straying to her mouth. He'd hoped to find he was wrong, but the fact remained that last night's attempt to quell any nerves over upcoming physical contact had backfired miserably. One kiss, and now he kept imagining a second and a third. His gaze strayed to her open collar. With only the top button left undone, he could only make out the hollow of her throat. Since when did he find that part of a woman's body so arousing? He watched her swallow and other sorts of intimate activities an engaged couple—or any consenting couple—would enjoy popped into his mind. Activities that would take place in a bedroom with the door closed and without the barrier of clothes or the bother of inhibitions.

Disturbed and aroused at the direction his

thoughts kept taking, he had to exhale slowly between his teeth. Even then, a portion of his pent-up groan escaped.

"Am I boring you yet?" Elizabeth inquired.

"Sorry. Not at all. In fact, quite the opposite. I'm fascinated," he admitted truthfully. He forced his gaze from her lips again. "That is, with what you do here. It's…fascinating."

If only he'd left it at that. But he lifted his hand to her face, and brushed his fingers over the slope of her cheek before tucking some hair behind her ear. He'd done something similar while they'd stood next to her car the previous evening. Though her hair was back to being stick-straight today, it was just as soft, and blessedly free of the sticky hairspray and comb teasing the women of his acquaintance tended to use in abundance.

"Thomas?"

He lowered his hand. "I was wondering…" He let the thought go unfinished since it was heading to boggy territory. He needed to keep their interaction professional, even if everything about their agreement was rooted in being personal. He cleared his throat. "Will it be possible to meet again this evening? We have a lot yet to learn about one another."

"I suppose so."

"Maybe I could come by your place, bring some Chinese food? Do you like Chinese?"

"M-my place?"

It sounded so much more damning when she said it, especially since her eyebrows were raised in alarm. So, he amended with an easy smile, "I'm eager to meet Howie."

The door had barely closed behind Thomas when Mel grabbed Elizabeth by the arm and began peppering her with questions.

"Okay, what exactly is going on? He looked like he was really into you. Not that I was spying or anything. I mean, the door to the main meeting room has a glass panel in it after all."

"Nothing is going on." Elizabeth wasn't trying to lie or be evasive with her friend. The truth was, she was having a hard time processing the events of the past twenty-four hours.

"He caressed your cheek."

A simple touch to which Elizabeth's entire body had overreacted foolishly. Indeed, just recalling it caused gooseflesh to prick her arms now.

For her benefit even more than Mel's she said flatly, "It's not what it seems. Nothing about it is."

"Really? It seemed pretty romantic to me." Mel crossed her arms. "Men don't touch women like that unless they're interested in more than making some sort of charitable contribution, worthy cause notwithstanding, sweetie. If you don't get that you've been off the dating circuit for far too long."

"They do in this instance," Elizabeth noted wryly. She glanced at her wrist again.

"Your watch still isn't there," Mel pointed out. "Now you've got me really curious. You're acting all air-headed. That's not like you at all."

"It's a long story, one you'll want to dissect, and we have clients coming in a few minutes." Besides, Elizabeth wanted to dissect it first.

"Fine." Mel sighed. "We'll talk about this at length over lunch, but for now, give me the abridged version."

Elizabeth sucked in a breath. "Thomas has agreed to make a personal donation to our campaign, a large one that will match the one coming from Waverly Enterprises."

Mel's expression barely flickered. "And?"

"You could at least act excited about that. We'll be meeting our goal."

"I am glad. Yay, us." Mel flashed a grin that was gone almost as fast as it appeared. Then she cocked her head to one side. "And?"

"He needs a favor. Yes, that's all it is. He needs a favor."

"You do realize that when I said to give me the abridged version, I didn't mean for you to speak in some sort of code," Mel replied dryly.

Elizabeth took another deep breath. "Okay, here's the long and the short of it. He needs a fiancée. More precisely, he needs a woman to act as his fiancée, just for this weekend when he goes to visit his grandmother."

Her friend's eyes widened. "Did you say *fiancée*?"

"*Act* is the key word here," Elizabeth stressed. "He's asked me to *act* as his fiancée. He's not interested in me in that way at all."

Despite that bit of clarification, her friend grabbed her wrist none too gently and pulled her toward the office. "Our clients can wait. I need you to start at the beginning and tell me everything."

The closer it came to the time to meet Elizabeth, the more unsettled Thomas became. It didn't make sense, yet it did. While he never was nervous before a date, when it came to an important business deal? Yes, occasionally. So that part fit. But he didn't slap on cologne before business meetings, no matter how vital they were. Nor did he change his clothes—twice—and even then worry about his appearance and what signals it might send to the other party. Too casual? Too formal? In the end, he wound up back in the same herringbone jacket, shirt and pants he'd worn to her office.

In the right front pocket, he'd tucked the box holding the engagement ring his father had given his mother more than three decades before. It was a pretty ring, more old-fashioned than timeless because of its carved white-gold setting. The diamond was a half-carat, round brilliant cut. It had come to be in Thomas's possession only after his father had pawned it to buy more liquor during one of his mad binges when Thomas was a child. He'd saved up his pennies and bought it back, able to afford it only because the shopkeeper's wife was sentimental. He'd kept it all these years, not to give to his own glowing bride-to-be someday, but as a reminder of the pain that kind of love and commitment carried.

On the way to her house he picked up the Chinese food he'd ordered ahead of time. Since he hadn't thought to ask Elizabeth her preference, he'd gone with a few options: one sweet and sour, a basic chicken stir-fry and, since he was fond of a little bite, something off the Szechwan side of the menu. Coming out of the restaurant, he spied the florist shop next door. A cart full of bundled fresh flowers was parked out front.

Women liked flowers. In Thomas's experience, they were especially fond of roses, attaching all sorts of meaning to them, especially when they were red and long-stemmed and came in a ribbon-tied box. With that in mind, he picked out a simple bouquet of white daisies in a cone of cellophane. They made a suitable hostess gift.

He drove slowly to Elizabeth's house, taking a mental inventory of all that he hoped to learn during the evening ahead. How her skin felt and what her hair smelled like were off the list. Instead, he needed to find out basic things, such as her date of birth and family background. Were her parents still alive? Were they together? Where did they live and was she on good terms with them? Did she have any siblings? If so, their names and ages, etc.

Should he ask about ex-boyfriends? He swallowed. Or…ex-husbands? No, he didn't want to go there. Her romantic history was of no importance to him, at least where Nana Jo was concerned, which made it difficult to explain the odd twist in his gut whenever he thought about Elizabeth sharing a bed with someone else.

He stopped for a traffic light, waited for it to turn green. When it did, he shifted more than the car's gears. His focus was now on the very safe topic of her education. The problem was, he already knew which university she'd attended, what discipline she'd studied while there and what she'd opted to do with her life upon graduation. Okay, that left her spare time. What did she do when she wasn't working? What were her hobbies and interests?

What were her vices?

On a groan, Thomas switched on the radio, flipped the station until he found some mind-emptying, bass-thumping rock and listened to music for the remainder of the drive.

Fifteen minutes later, he turned on Clement Avenue, going slow, not only out of deference to the children who were outside playing, but also so that he could read the address numbers.

Elizabeth lived in one of the city's older neighborhoods. As such, the street was lined with mature trees and with homes that, while generally well-kept, were in need of a little updating. Hers was no exception, Thomas thought, as he pulled his car to a stop in front of a small bungalow. The faded green aluminum awnings that covered the porch and front windows harkened back a good half century. They reminded him of the awnings that had graced his parents' house. The home he'd grown up in until the accident that had taken one life and irrevocably changed three others.

Nana Jo had moved into the house with Thomas during his father's first unsuccessful stint in rehab, appalled to discover that her son had removed every last trace of his late wife from the rooms. Gone were the photos, the mementos, even some of the furniture that Lynn had purchased. Indeed, gone in some places was the plaster, where Hoyt had smashed his fist through the wall as he'd raged against God and fate, and drank himself into oblivion while his young son watched, frightened and baffled.

Four more stints in rehab followed before Thomas started middle school. At first, Hoyt came home between his stays at Brighter Futures Addiction Recovery. Sober, he was full of apologies and promises, but also weighted down with guilt and the dooming grief that he was never able to shake. Eventually, he stopped going to rehab and he stopped coming home. Thomas would have wound up a ward of the state, the house lost to back taxes, had it not been for Nana Jo.

She had been, and in many ways remained, Thomas's rock.

Gradually, she'd brought more of her belongings over from her own house across town. Doilies appeared on the living room tables, knickknacks on the empty shelves that bracketed the kitchen window. A cheery, hand-crocheted afghan was draped over the back of the sofa, and new linens appeared on the beds. The walls were patched and repainted. The house became a home again and Thomas's busted-up life was put back together, too.

Nana Jo sold the house after he left to attend college and then purchased her condo in Charlevoix, which had no yard work or outside maintenance for her to do. He still missed that little house sometimes, but only because of the good memories that Nana Jo had taken such care to preserve and later create.

Dated or not, Elizabeth's house managed to be every bit as inviting as his boyhood abode thanks to a vivid assortment of flowers that spilled from a pair of large pots on either side of the front walk. From one side of the porch, a fern dripped from a hanging basket. The word *Welcome* was printed on the mat, but it didn't need to be.

Home, he thought. And that word stayed in his mind, even after the woman appeared in the door.

CHAPTER FIVE

AT HOWIE'S barking, Elizabeth peeked out the window and spied Thomas standing on the sidewalk. He was gazing at the house, a far-off expression on his face. She could only imagine what he was thinking.

He was fifteen minutes early. Again. At least this time she was ready for him. She'd left work early so that she could let Howie out to work off the worst of a day's worth of pent-up energy, and so that she could tidy up her house. Of course, her small bungalow didn't need much tidying.

She liked order. Growing up with her free-wheeling parents, who'd eschewed home ownership for a more nomadic lifestyle, Elizabeth now thrived on the stability of knowing where she would be sleeping each night and that the bed would be made with fresh linens. Small things like having a well-stocked refrigerator and the appliances necessary to make a hot meal added a sense of security that her childhood had lacked. She wasn't completely boring, but she had a clear plan for her future. Surprises were fine as long as she was prepared to deal with any consequences that came along with them. Her parents were no good at dealing with consequences.

She loved them dearly, but she didn't want to be anything like them, except where their relationship with one another was concerned. Skeet and Delphine were quirky, oblivious and downright irresponsible, but they loved one another without reservation or condition.

So, she'd been looking for a man who was nothing like her father; but, at his core, very much like her father. That is to say, capable of deep love and lifelong commitment. What she hadn't been looking for was a man like Thomas Waverly, but that was exactly who now stood on her doorstep holding a bag of Chinese food and a clutch of daisies, and wearing a forced smile as Howie growled menacingly at him from behind her.

"Howie!" she admonished. To Thomas, she said, "He's really nothing but a big baby."

Her "big baby" looked ready to jump through the screen door at her guest, which was odd. He'd never had this reaction to company in the past.

"I'm sorry. I don't know what's gotten into him. He's never acted like this before."

"Apparently, I bring out the worst in him." Thomas laughed tightly.

"It's probably just that not many men come to my door...lately."

Thomas eyed the dog and drew a different conclusion. "He's protective of you. It's a good quality in a dog."

"I guess so." She reached for Howie's collar, pulling him back. "I'll just go put him in my bedroom."

"I'd appreciate it," Thomas said.

When she came back down the hall, he was still standing on her porch. "All clear?"

"All clear."

She held open the door and then led him back to her small kitchen. Its harvest-gold appliances and battered Formica countertop were hopelessly out-of-date. As were the white cabinets that had been painted so many times that some of them refused to close properly. Renovation was on her to-do list, but she had neither the time nor the money to tackle any serious home improvement for the foreseeable future.

"It's very retro in here," Thomas commented.

"Retro. Yes. That's exactly the vibe I was going for."

"You have a good sense of humor," he accused on a smile as he set the cartons of food on the small, bar-height bistro set that was tucked into the corner of the tiny kitchen. "A dry one."

"I guess I do," she agreed. "Are those for me?"

He was still holding the flowers.

"Yes."

He all but thrust them into her hands. Elizabeth gave the bouquet a sniff. Daisies didn't emit the lush fragrance of, say, carnations or lilies, but she found their subtle earthiness refreshing. "Daisies are my favorite flower."

"They're a hostess gift," he blurted out with curious intensity.

"Well, they're lovely. Thank you." As she pulled a vase from a cupboard and put them in water, Elizabeth said, "Has anyone ever told you that you have wonderful manners?"

"All the time." He removed his jacket and placed it over the back of his chair before taking his seat. "It was my grandmother's doing."

"I like your grandmother."

"Just wait until you meet her."

Both of them grew serious then. That was the objective. For Elizabeth to meet his grandmother and pass muster as his supposed bride-to-be.

"Do you think she'll like me?" Elizabeth realized it was a silly question as soon as she asked it. She shook her head. "She already does, doesn't she? I mean, the fabricated version of me." It hit her then. "Beth. That's my name as far as she knows."

"It is." He tilted his head to one side. "Do you mind being called Beth?"

"It's only for a little while. I'll get used to it." She shrugged and went to get plates and utensils. She was quite proficient with chopsticks, but she grabbed a fork for Thomas just in case.

He didn't appear satisfied with her answer. "You know, the more I get to know you, the less you look like a Beth."

"Oh?" Curious, she asked, "What does a Beth look like?"

He flushed slightly. "It doesn't matter. I'll call you Elizabeth. It suits you better anyway."

"And how do you know that?" she challenged.

"I...I don't." His mouth snapped shut and he was silent a moment. Then he asked, "What kind of movies do you like?"

His quick switch in topics baffled her. "Movies?"

"We're getting to know one another, re-member? That's the whole point of this eve-ning."

Of course it was.

"Movies," she repeated. "I don't go to the theater often. To be perfectly honest, I'm not much for first-run films. I can't name any of the big stars currently walking the red carpet at premieres and award shows." In a teasing tone, she asked, "Does that make me a Beth or an Elizabeth?"

"It makes you a smart-ass," he shot back, after which he immediately apologized for cursing.

Ah, those impeccable manners of his. She didn't want to acknowledge what a turn-on she found them to be. She busied herself set-ting the table.

"So, you like old movies," he prodded.

"Mainly Alfred Hitchcock films, although I'm also a sucker for anything that stars Kath-arine Hepburn and Spencer Tracy."

"No way."

"What? You like Tracy and Hepburn?"

"No. Hitchcock. The man was a genius," Thomas replied solemnly. "*Dial M for Murder* is my favorite. You?"

"*North by Northwest,*" she replied without hesitation.

"Let me guess. Cary Grant has something to do with your preference?" He opened the containers and scooped out a clump of white rice onto each of their plates.

"Well, maybe just a little," she admitted on a grin as she levered herself onto the chair opposite his. "He's also the reason I love *To Catch a Thief*."

"Grace Kelly." Thomas sighed. "She starred in that one with him."

"She starred in few Hitchcock movies, including your favorite." Elizabeth arched a brow. "Am I sensing the reason behind your preference?"

"Guilty. So, what about *Psycho*? Fan of that one?" He made a slashing-knife motion with the corresponding sound effect that had turned the simple act of showering into the stuff of nightmares.

She couldn't help it. She shuddered. "I saw it once, as an adult no less, and that was enough for me. I found it a little too intense."

"Twice here. Also as an adult. Both times while out with women. Based on my dates' reactions, they also found it intense. I didn't mind." His smile, accompanied as it was by a pair of bobbing eyebrows, had her laughing.

Feeling the need to redeem herself, Elizabeth said, "I've watched *The Birds* again and again."

"A cult classic," Thomas agreed.

She helped herself to some Kung Pao chicken. "I will admit that, as a kid, it made me look at seagulls in a whole new light. Going to the beach was a traumatic experience for a time."

He went for the Kung Pao chicken as well once she set the carton back on the table.

"Definitely dry." At her blank expression, he added, "Your sense of humor." He motioned with the serving spoon. "Back to *The Birds*, how about that scene at the elementary school? All those crows perching on the monkey bars?"

"Creepy in the extreme."

"Wasn't it, though? I was nine the first time I saw that movie. It was on television one rainy Saturday afternoon, and I watched it while Nana Jo was hosting her bridge club. I was awake all night long."

"I was eleven. Slept on the floor in my parents' room for a week."

"I wouldn't admit this to just anyone, but seeing as how you and I are engaged…" He shrugged. "I slept on my grandmother's floor for two." They both laughed. "It came to a

head when she tried to take me to the play-
ground and I begged to stay home."

"What did she say?"

"Well, she was mystified."

"Understandable."

"But she didn't press." His smile turned
nostalgic. "That's her way. Or at least it was
back then. She's run out of patience, apparently. As for *The Birds*, I eventually confessed
all."

"And?" Elizabeth broke apart the wooden
chopsticks that had come with their meal.

"Nana Jo took me to the local pet store and
subjected me to an hour in the bird aisle. Even
with every last one of those birds confined in
cages, it was terrifying."

"Did she really do that?"

Thomas glanced at the fork she'd set out for
him before picking up his pair of chopsticks
and breaking them apart. "She felt it was the
best way for me to confront my fear. In fact,
she bought me a cockatiel."

"Did it work?"

"Yes. I was cured thereafter, but hopelessly
hooked on Hitchcock." He attempted to pick
up a bite of his meal. Chicken and rice slipped
from between the chopsticks. His expression
reflected his dismay.

"What did you name the bird?"

His frown of a moment before turned into a sly grin. "What do you think?"

"Hitchcock."

"Exactly. Confronting fear head on, remember?"

They both laughed. Then Elizabeth took a bite of the food. The hot peppers in the Kung Pao chicken made her eyes water, even as her tongue caught fire. She set her chopsticks aside and fanned her face.

"Oh, my God! I need a glass of water." She scooted off her chair. "I never thought to ask if you wanted something to drink. I have wine, Cabernet Sauvignon." It was a date-night staple, or so Mel always claimed. Elizabeth added, "Or some diet cola if you'd prefer."

"Water's fine."

"Tap?"

"With a couple ice cubes if you've got 'em."

When she returned to the table with their glasses, he was again struggling to pick up a piece of chicken with his chopsticks. This one wound up in his lap after leaving a trail of sauce and bits of rice down the front of his shirt. His smile was sheepish, and all the more appealing because of it, as he blotted the fabric with a napkin. "I'm not as good at this as you are, I'm afraid."

"But you just keep trying."

"That's me. Once I set my mind to doing something, I don't give up easily."

"I'm the same way. Determined." She laughed. "Mel calls it being stubborn."

"I guess we both are, then."

His smile was warm, yet she had to suppress a shiver. Elizabeth cleared her throat.

"You're holding them wrong." She picked up her pair again and demonstrated. Even though Thomas did better this time, his grip was still a little off.

"That's an improvement, but it's more like this." She reached over to adjust the placement of his middle finger between the two sticks. Just that little bit of contact sent a spark of heat zipping up her spine, every bit as potent as the previous evening's kiss. She snatched her hand back and glanced up to find him watching her. His dark eyes were narrowed and had grown hooded.

Was he recalling that kiss as well?

She was being foolish, she decided, when he made a couple of pinching motions in the air.

"I think I've got it," he declared before attempting to pick up another piece of chicken. This time he brought it to his mouth without incident. He raised his empty chopsticks in triumph afterward.

"Very good," she said.

"Well, you're a good teacher."

She wrinkled her nose at the compliment. "Nah. You're a smart man from what I've observed. You would have figured it out for yourself eventually."

"Still, you deserve a reward." He picked up a second piece of chicken and, after making sure it wasn't going to fall from the chopsticks, offered it to her.

Elizabeth must have lost her mind, because she leaned closer and opened her mouth. All the while, her gaze stayed on Thomas rather than the prize he offered. Even as her lips closed around the chopsticks and heat—both that inspired by the hot peppers in the recipe and that inspired by need—wound through her, she maintained eye contact.

"I wouldn't have taken you for the sort of woman who enjoyed Kung Pao chicken," he said slowly. "It's got a lot of kick, especially from the restaurant I patronize."

"Hence the sweet and sour pork and chicken stir-fry," she replied.

His smile was lightning quick and appealing. "I was hedging my bets with a good assortment."

"That was very thoughtful, but as it turns out there was no need. I like spice. Lots of it, in fact." She sipped her water, took her time swallowing. Regardless, the heat not only remained, but also burned even hotter.

That studious look was back on his face. "I have a feeling there's a lot more to you, Elizabeth Morris, than first meets the eye."

She held his gaze. "The same is true for most people, I think."

It was definitely true for Thomas. She'd had him pegged as a smooth operator based on his handsome face and admitted commitment-phobia. Add in that kiss and she'd known he was vastly experienced when it came to casual physical relationships, making him exactly the sort of man any woman who valued keeping her heart whole knew to avoid. But that opinion shifted once she figured in his manners and his deep love for his grandmother. Just as she had the night before, Elizabeth found herself marveling at all of his layers and almost wishing they were involved in the sort of relationship that allowed one to delve deeper, explore and, eventually, see more.

"What you're telling me is you can't judge a book by its cover," he said.

"Am I sensing some regrets? Perhaps I'm not the right woman for this…job after all."

"No. No regrets." But he was frowning when he said, "I have a feeling you're perfect."

CHAPTER SIX

THEY talked throughout their meal about the inconsequential things that ultimately helped people get to know one another. Little by little, more of the true Elizabeth Morris emerged. As Thomas already had surmised, there was far more to her than first met the eye. And he wasn't completely comfortable with the woman now seated across from him.

He'd meant it when he'd said earlier that he had the feeling she was perfect. Not just for the role he wanted her to play, either. She was funny, interesting and smart, definitely. And he knew from that kiss that, under different circumstances, he wouldn't mind pursuing a more intimate relationship with her. But that would have to wait, assuming she felt the same way. Right now it was business. Even if it also came with a few perks, he decided, as his gaze slid to her mouth. As long as they were on the same page, he might as well as enjoy them.

He rounded up the last morsel of chicken on his plate and grinned in satisfaction when it stayed between his chopsticks. After eating it, he motioned across the room. "Tell me about that picture on your refrigerator door."

She glanced over. Amusement was apparent in her eyes and her voice when she replied, "The one of Mel and me shrieking like a pair of loons?"

"Exactly."

"I'm a roller-coaster junkie," she admitted, reaching up to adjust the band that held her hair back from her face. "I'm guessing that comes as a surprise to you, too."

"Guilty." While he would have pictured her holding on for dear life as the car crested the summit and plunged over, he saw proof to the contrary affixed to the refrigerator. The photo of her and the young woman he'd met at Literacy Liaisons showed Elizabeth in the front seat of the first car, slim arms waving over her head, a delighted grin flashing over her face.

"Well, I am. The steeper, the faster, the more winding the better." She said it with pride and just a little defiance.

"When and where was that taken?"

"Last summer. Mel and I took some of our

younger clients on a field trip to an amusement park in Ohio," she told him. "That particular coaster was new and billed as the highest and fastest one in the Midwest. Mel dared me to go on it and take that first plunge hands-free." Now her smile was every bit as smug as it was nostalgic.

"Can't turn down a dare?" His mouth began to water. He blamed it on the spices that were still making his tongue sting.

"Sure I can. But not one where I know I can do it."

"Dang." He snapped his fingers in mock dismay. "Another one of my misconceptions busted."

"Besides, there was an ice-cream cone riding on my saying yes."

"Ice cream. I like ice cream." His gaze was on her mouth and his own was watering again. This time, there was no denying the exact cause.

"Who doesn't?"

"What flavor do you prefer?"

"Vanilla." Elizabeth cocked her head to one side. "Before you condemn me for being boring—"

"Never." He meant it. He was finding her way too enchanting to be bored.

"Good." She offered a quick smile before

continuing. "Vanilla is my favorite because it's the most versatile flavor of ice cream out there. As such, it offers one a chance to get creative."

"I guess I never thought of it that way before," he replied truthfully.

"Most people haven't, but they should. Buy a half gallon of vanilla ice cream and you can add whatever you want and create the exact flavor you're after."

"Practical," he agreed.

Her frown told him she didn't quite care for the description, even before she said, "I prefer to think of it as being flexible, maybe even a little imaginative. Add fresh strawberries, chocolate syrup, caramel, peanuts, what have you and you've crafted a new flavor."

"The possibilities are endless." Suddenly, he was seeing vanilla in a whole new light, just as he'd already begun to see Elizabeth differently.

They chatted about coasters and ice cream for the remainder of their meal. When they finished eating, he helped her carry their dishes to the sink. She tried to shoo him back to his seat.

"There's no need. Really. You're my guest."

"Actually, I'm your fiancé, remember?" He chose not to ponder how easily the word rolled off his tongue. "My grandmother was a stickler when it came to household chores. From the first day she came to live with us, she drilled into me the importance of cleaning up after myself."

"Smart woman."

He nodded. "That bit of instruction has served me well. I may be a bachelor, but my house isn't a pigsty."

Her brows rose. "Cleaning lady?"

"Well, yeah. But she only comes every other week."

Elizabeth grinned as she finished rinsing off their plates and stacking them on the counter next to the sink. Afterward, she turned toward him, her expression both innocent and beguiling when she asked, "So, now what?"

Now, there was a question. Usually after dinner with a woman one of two things happened. If it was early in a relationship, they engaged in prolonged foreplay. If they'd been dating awhile and were mutually agreeable, they skipped all pretense and headed to the nearest bedroom. Maybe it was just as well that Elizabeth's was currently occupied with one very large and not so friendly canine.

He glanced at his watch. It wasn't quite nine. The last time he'd ended an evening out with a member of the opposite sex this early, he'd been a teenager with a curfew. Besides, they had barely scratched the surface. He didn't know nearly enough about Elizabeth to satisfy either his grandmother's or his own curiosity.

"I'm eager to hear more revelations. What other dark secrets are you hiding?" He said it in jest, but for a second she looked...guilty?

He must have imagined it, he decided. Because a moment later she was grinning gamely when she announced, "Well, I like to play poker."

"Poker?"

"It's not like I'm a contender for one of those televised tournaments where the stakes are huge or anything, but I enjoy the game." She rinsed out their glasses. "More water?"

"After that revelation, I think I could use a glass of that wine you offered me earlier."

He uncorked the bottle while she got out a couple of what appeared to be handblown goblets.

"Fancy," he commented as he poured.

"They were a gift from a client, one of our first. Cassidy McClurg. She's on track now to earn her sommelier certification. Her dream is to work someday at a top New York restaurant. I think she's well on her way."

"To Literacy Liaisons and changing lives."

He handed Elizabeth one of the glasses and then clinked his against it.

They adjourned to her small livingroom then. Since the windows were open, he could hear the crickets chirping outside and sundry other noises associated with nightfall in a neighborhood. He missed those sounds now that his windows were always closed with the central air-conditioning humming.

Like the kitchen, the room needed updating. The carpet, a nondescript brown color, was faded in places with well-worn paths from the postage-stamp-sized foyer to the kitchen and the hallway that led to the bedrooms. But the place was tidy. And homey thanks to all of the little touches that, quite frankly, were lacking in the sprawling house he'd lived in for more than half a decade.

He settled into the recliner after Elizabeth sat on the love seat. Their positions made for easier conversation. That's what he told himself anyway, since the empty cushion next to her looked way too inviting.

"Let's get back to you and poker."

It turned out she played mainly at charity fundraising events and had never been to any of Michigan's American Indian tribe-run casinos, let alone the huge gambling venues found in Las Vegas. But she knew the difference between a full house and a straight and, given that serene, guileless expression of hers, he'd bet she was a pro at bluffing.

Still, she threw him for a loop when she added, "Mel, a couple other friends and I have been getting together about once a month for the past couple years. We play for bragging rights mostly."

A bunch of women playing poker on a regular basis? "Please tell me you don't sit around smoking cigars and talking sports, too?"

Amusement shimmered in her eyes. "Sports, sometimes. If it's college football season, Mel and I usually have a side bet going. She went to State like me, but she's still a Wolverine fan. Family tradition."

"I'm surprised her family didn't toss her from the fold when she decided to attend State then," he teased.

"She had a full-ride scholarship. It was kind of hard for her parents to be upset with her choice in universities when they didn't have to pick up the tab for a Big Ten school's tuition." Elizabeth shrugged. "Not that my scholarship stopped *my* parents from being upset."

"You had a full-ride scholarship to State and they were unhappy about it?" he asked incredulously.

"Not exactly a full ride, but enough that I

was able to afford my four years there when supplemented with student loans. My parents' objections were more…generalized." She shook her head. Before he could ask what she meant by that, Elizabeth said, "Back to Mel, she chose State because it has a strong program in her field of study."

"Which was?"

"Package engineering."

"So, she went from designing the packaging for products to vetting literacy volunteers?" He scratched his chin, not quite able to connect the dots. "I'm not seeing the correlation between the two professions."

"That's because there is none. Mel was great at her job and made a lot of money at it, but she didn't like what she was doing or where she was doing it." Before he could ask, Elizabeth supplied, "San Francisco."

"Yeah," he replied dryly. "I can see how living in the 'City by the Bay' would be a real downer, especially in the middle of winter when we're buried in snow here."

Elizabeth laughed. The sound was lyrical and the way her face lit was, well…he liked it. A lot.

"She didn't miss Michigan's weather, Mr. Smarty Pants. She missed the people here."

"Mr. Smarty Pants?" he repeated with brows raised.

Thomas couldn't recall a single woman who had ever referred to him as such. Well, except for his grandmother. The young women of his acquaintance had other, far more flattering pet names for him. Names that usually couldn't be repeated in polite company since they had to do with things that had occurred behind closed bedroom doors. Those names had helped stroke his ego. Yet he found himself more amused than offended by Elizabeth's assessment. Her engaging grin probably had something to do with it.

"You think you have all the answers." The charge was leveled too lightly to be an accusation.

"Do I now?"

"Just an observation." She shrugged and reached for the wineglass she'd set on the coffee table.

"My guess is you were one of the things your friend missed about Michigan."

"Well, we are BFFs." Elizabeth smiled fondly.

That had come through loud and clear when he'd been introduced. As had her friend's protectiveness. She might be as petite as Elizabeth, but Thomas got the feeling she would cheerfully scratch out his eyes if she thought he'd hurt Elizabeth.

Elizabeth was saying, "Long story short, she ditched a lucrative career in the corporate world for something she finds more personally satisfying."

"Now she uses her power for good," he teased.

"More like for the greater good."

"I'd say it worked out for both of you, then. Does she, um, know about our arrangement?"

"Yes. BFFs, remember?"

"Right."

Elizabeth nibbled her lower lip thoughtfully for a second. "Can I ask you something?"

"Of course." Thomas lifted his shoulders in a shrug. Because he felt the need to remind himself, he told her, "That's whole the point of this evening, Elizabeth. We're supposed to be getting to know one another. So, ask away."

"Do you…are you…? It's just that Mel is very…" She let out a bemused laugh and re-adjusted her headband. Before it was back in place, blond hair cascaded about her face. He liked it better that way. "This is really awkward."

Which made Thomas all the more intrigued. "Why don't you say it fast, like pulling off a bandage?"

"Okay." But she still took a moment during which she sucked in a deep breath. "It's just that, to me at least, Mel seems more your type. Yet, when you met her earlier today, you didn't pay very much attention to her."

More his type? Hmm. Thomas supposed that, except for her petite stature, Mel Sutton was in league with the sort of women he tended to date. At least her physical appearance. She was sexy and beautiful. Oddly enough, he hadn't been attracted to her. And even if he had been, since he'd gone to Literacy Liaisons to see Elizabeth, his pseudo-fiancée, it would have been impolite to openly ogle her friend.

"I didn't mean to offend her," he began.

Elizabeth shook her head. The band loosened again. "You didn't offend her. I was just surprised that, well, that you didn't—"

She stopped abruptly. Thomas had a feeling he knew why. Now, he was a little offended. "That I didn't what, Elizabeth? Hit on her?"

"Well, no." She moistened her lips, readjusted her headband again.

He was tempted to pull it off completely. He didn't care for the prim look. He liked her hair better loose so that, if he wanted to, he could run his fingers through it.

"Then what?"

"Okay. I did think that maybe you would… hit on her, to use your term. And, quite frankly, I wouldn't have been surprised."

Oh, he was definitely offended. "Because I'm a lecherous pig."

She blinked at his bald statement. "No! It's just that Mel's gorgeous."

"So?"

On a frown, she asked, "Are you going to sit there and tell me you didn't notice?"

"No. I'm not blind, so, sure I noticed, just like I would notice a gorgeous sunset or a stunning piece of artwork. I appreciate beauty in all things. Everyone does. That's human nature. But I am capable of some restraint, you know," he finished dryly.

He thought that would be the end of it. Subject closed. It wasn't.

Chin notched up, Elizabeth declared, "Just so you know, Mel is every bit as pretty on the inside as she is on the outside. She's not merely an attractive package."

"Even if she is a packaging engineer."

His attempt at a joke fell miserably flat.

"Mel is smart and funny and generous, not that most men ever figure that out or even bother to try."

Her vehement defense of her best friend

might have been touching if it hadn't also highlighted Elizabeth's own insecurities.

"So are you…every bit as pretty on the inside as you are on the outside, from what I can tell." Indeed, the more he saw, the more he liked. And the more attractive he found her to be.

That disturbed him a little. What was it his dad had said just prior to going on one of his drunken binges? That he'd fallen in love with Thomas's mother not in spite of her quirks and imperfections, but because of them.

Elizabeth was quick to disagree with his assessment. "I'm not pretty. I'm not ugly or anything, but…" She fiddled with the headband again. "I'm rather plain."

"Plain?" Did she really think so? With that lush mouth and those rich, dark eyes? Not a chance. He might be out of line, but he reached over and tugged the headband free, tossing it on the coffee table like a gauntlet. A cascade of satiny tresses fell forward, all but obscuring her face before he pushed them back. "From where I'm sitting you're very pretty," he challenged.

A blush stained her cheeks as she fiddled with the stem of her wineglass.

It had been a long time since Thomas had been around a woman who became flustered from a simple compliment. "By the way, Elizabeth…?"

"Yes?"

"I'm not most men."

CHAPTER SEVEN

As if she needed reminding on that score. Quite frankly, Thomas was unlike anyone she'd ever met—personally or professionally. And that was saying a lot given all of the doors upon which she'd knocked during the past several months to raise funds for the endowment.

She still wasn't quite sure how to act around him in part because their relationship was professional and personal at the same time. It didn't help that she found him so appealing. But that was superficial. It was based on sexual chemistry, she reminded herself. Beyond his good looks and his love for his grandmother, what did she truly know about him? If she was to pull off her part as his fiancée—and that was her only motive here—she needed to know more about him.

Much more than that she found him too handsome and charming for her peace of mind.

Besides, she'd rather he be the one in the hot seat.

"You know, I just realized that while I've been telling you a lot about myself, I don't know nearly enough about you except that you matriculated from Michigan and have the good sense to be a fan of Alfred Hitchcock."

"What else do you want to know?"

Where to start? Favorite color? Favorite dessert? Where he went on his last vacation? How old he was when he stopped believing in Santa Claus? Benign topics, all, and definitely the sorts of things a fiancée should or would be expected to know.

But the question she heard herself ask was "When did your last relationship end?" Followed quickly by "You're not involved with someone right now, are you?"

Last night, Thomas hadn't kissed like a man who was stepping out on his girlfriend, but then their situation was hardly normal. The kiss had been for effect. It was intended to put them both at ease, not that the objective had been achieved as far as Elizabeth was concerned.

"I'm not seeing anyone."

She let out a breath that she hadn't been aware she was holding. "Good. I mean, it would be awkward otherwise. For her. And, well, for me. I'd hate to be the 'other woman,' even if only in theory." She ordered herself to stop babbling and cleared her throat. "And as for my other question, what's the answer to that?"

Thomas's expression turned oddly introspective as he studied his wine. After taking a sip, he said, "I don't know that I'd necessarily call it a relationship, though it was exclusive for as long as it lasted." He looked up, his gaze locked with hers. "When I'm seeing someone, Elizabeth, I'm faithful."

"We're not really 'seeing each other,'" she said before she could wonder if he even meant to apply monogamy to their situation. Hoping to lighten the moment, she added, "I mean, could it even be considered cheating if said cheating involved a fictitious fiancée?"

At his lifted brow, she figured she'd made things clear as mud with her attempt at humor.

"Fictitious or not, I won't be dating during our…engagement."

That should have been reassuring, except that it called to mind another question Elizabeth realized she hadn't yet gotten around to asking. "How long will that be? You never actually said."

He frowned. "I don't know the exact length of time, but I'll only need your, um, services—" He must have found that word as unsavory as she did. "That is, your cooperation for this weekend. Nana Jo just wants to meet my fiancée. And, given the distance between here and Charlevoix, it's not like she's going to be expecting us to drive up for Sunday dinner each week."

"Oh. Good." And that was good, she reminded herself, when she experienced a foolish twinge of disappointment.

"I won't withhold my personal donation to Literacy Liaisons until our 'breakup,' if that's what you're worried about. The check will be on your desk the first business day after the holiday weekend."

Waverly Enterprises's check had been received not long after he'd left her office earlier in the day. Already, it had been deposited into the agency's special bank account.

"I wasn't worried." She'd forgotten all about the check during the past couple of hours, but she would do well to remember that Thomas's generous donation was the reason she was doing this. Even so, she nibbled her bottom lip and asked, "So, how long did it last?"

"What?"

"Your last relationship."

"Oh." He appeared to do some quick

mental calculations. "I guess it was nearly two months."

"Wow. A whole two months. And you managed to stay faithful the entire time."

"Sarcasm. Hmm." His expression turned bemused and he wagged a finger in her direction. "I wouldn't have thought you capable of it."

Elizabeth rarely resorted to sarcasm or to sarcastic humor. In fact, she found it a bit of a turnoff, one of the main reasons she didn't watch many television sitcoms, which relied on it so heavily for their laughs.

"I apologize for the sarcasm."

"No need."

"There is," she insisted. "My comment was rude."

Thomas's smile was rueful. "But not completely unwarranted or off base. As I told you last night, I'm not interested in commitment. So, I tend to end relationships quickly with the women I date. I prefer for things not to get too…"

"Intimate?"

"Messy."

"I see. And when was it that you ended things this last time?" she asked.

"Three weeks ago."

"Three weeks ago." Elizabeth resisted the

urge to whistle through her teeth. She didn't like the sound of that, though why it should matter she didn't know. Still, there was no denying that it did. It made her feel only marginally better that he'd been the one to end it. No pining going on, apparently. But three weeks? The scent of the woman's perfume was probably still lingering in his home. And on his linens.

"Is that a problem?" he asked.

"No. Why would it be?" Why, indeed?

"No hearts were broken, I can assure you," he said.

She slowly turned the stem of her wineglass. Gaze affixed to the deep red liquid, she asked quietly, "Have you ever had your heart broken?"

"No. Not once, which has been my objective." It was a curious thing to admit. Before she could question him on it, though, he said, "What about you?"

She thought about the guys she'd dated in the past. She wasn't as prolific a dater as Thomas apparently was, but she'd enjoyed a couple of long-term relationships, including one that had lasted more than a year. Things had progressed at a normal pace, though they'd never gotten past the point of exchanging keys, much less making promises to spend a lifetime together. Her heart had been dinged up afterward, but broken? She'd thought so at the time, but now…

"No."

"So, you've never been in love, either?"

"I guess not." That came as a sad revelation. After all, Elizabeth was pushing thirty.

But Thomas looked pleased. "Good. It's not worth it, you know."

"How can you say that when you just admitted that you've never been in love yourself?"

"Let's just say I know. I saw firsthand what it can do to people." He shook his head. "No thanks. I don't want to be that—"

"Vulnerable?"

"Foolish," he clarified.

He saw love as foolish? Perhaps she should have expected that since here he was trying to pass off a woman he barely knew as his fiancée. Still, it seemed…sad.

Thinking back on her own relationships now, she said, "I think it would be nice to be deeply in love with someone."

"In love? Yes. But you can't stay there." His tone was matter-of-fact.

"Why not? You don't think love can last?" She had her parents' example to prove otherwise. No marriage certificate bound them together, but their commitment was real.

But Thomas wasn't disagreeing. Not exactly. "It lasts. Unfortunately, it lasts beyond the grave."

"Should it have a time limit, an expiration date?"

"No. No." He shook his head, looking both lost and resolute. "It shouldn't, and it doesn't end. It lasts forever. It's a chronic condition, not a terminal one."

"I'm not sure I understand your objection, then."

"My dad loved my mother. Deeply." His tone was barely above a whisper when he added, "Desperately."

"And that's bad?"

"Not when she was alive, it wasn't." Half of his mouth lifted briefly before his lips thinned into a straight line. "My parents and I were involved in an accident when I was eight. Our car skidded off the road in a rainstorm and wound up upside down in a water-filled ravine."

His tone was flat, but his expression was haunted. So much so that it made Elizabeth ache for him. Ache for them all.

"Your mother didn't make it," Elizabeth guessed. Pieces of the puzzle started to fall into place. She didn't like the picture that was emerging.

He shook his head slowly. "For my grand-mother's benefit, my father claimed that she died instantly. But I was there."

Thomas said no more than that. He wasn't trying to be evasive. He simply wasn't capable of forcing the words past his lips and giving voice to a truth that had haunted him for more than two decades: Had the choice been left to his father, Hoyt would have saved his wife rather than his son.

But Thomas's mother hadn't given her husband the option. As murky water had gushed into the car through the broken windshield, and Hoyt had struggled to unbuckle her jammed seat belt, she'd batted his hands away and screamed, *Don't worry about me! Get Tommy out! Get Tommy out!*

"Oh, Thomas. I'm so sorry."

Elizabeth's sincere sympathy wasn't able to banish the hellish memories. Nothing was. He knew that from experience. But he couldn't deny that he found her concern soothing, set-tling.

"It's not something I like talking about it," he admitted. Even with Nana Jo, he preferred to steer clear of the subject. It was just too damned painful, for her as well, he figured, since she'd lost her only child.

"I understand. Ordinarily, I would consider this none of my business, but, given our unique set of circumstances…how did your grandmother come to raise you if your father is still alive?"

"My father's an alcoholic." Another admission he rarely shared. "He was what I'd call a social drinker before the accident. Afterward…" Thomas set the wine he'd barely touched on the coffee table. "He could down a fifth of whiskey in a day and then stumble to the store for more. He tried rehab, more than once. But I don't think his heart was in it. He was lost without my mother. He still is. And he's still drinking. Of that much I'm sure, even though I rarely see him."

Thomas glanced over, fully expecting to see pity in Elizabeth's eyes. It was there, along with something else, something that made him almost yearn for the comfort he knew she wanted to give him.

"It's hard when someone you love walks out of your life."

"I had no choice in the matter," Thomas heard himself say.

He swallowed thickly afterward. Even so, feelings welled up, helplessness chief among them. He'd had no say in his father's emotional and physical defection, just as he'd had no say in surviving the accident. *Get Tommy out!* How ironic that his mother's unconditional love had made him unlovable in his father's eyes. At least that was the way Thomas saw it.

Elizabeth said nothing. Instead, she came over and sat next to him on the love seat, angled toward him. Their knees bumped. She laid one of her small hands overtop of his, which were clenched tightly together in front of him. The gesture was one of comfort. Because that was what he knew he would find, he pulled away and stood.

"You know, it's getting late."

"Oh. I guess it is." She wasn't quite successful in hiding her bafflement.

"Thanks for dinner."

"You brought the Chinese," she pointed out.

"The company, then." He started for the door.

"You're welcome." But her smile was uncertain.

She followed him onto the porch. Outside, darkness was falling. Up and down the street, landscape lights were starting to click on. Elizabeth reached back into the house and flipped on the porch light, but it barely illuminated beyond the steps.

"Be careful getting to your car," she said as he started down her walk.

"I'm good." He waved and then made a liar of himself by tripping on the buckled pavement.

"Thomas—"

"I'm fine!"

"Good night," she called.

Rather than echo the sentiment, he halted midstep, turned around and returned to her, stopping one crumbling cement step shy of the porch where she still stood.

"Did you forget something?"

In his haste to leave, he almost had.

"My jacket." The engagement ring was in its pocket still. He would hand her the box and go. That way he'd be gone before he had to listen to her ooh and aah over it. She could put it on her own finger.

"It's in the kitchen."

He followed her back inside the tidy little home that still felt too welcoming for his peace of mind. But his gaze wasn't drawn to the furnishings or kitschy bric-a-brac. It was on her back, sliding south even as he ordered it to return to a safe point between her shoulder blades. She might not have a lot in the way of curves, but what she had filled out the seat of her pants well enough to make his mouth water. A groan slipped out as need surged in. She turned. The view from the front was just as appealing.

"Did you say something?"

Tell her no, get your jacket and go, he ordered silently. But what came out was her name. He stepped closer, until a mere whisper of space separated them. Then his hands were in her hair and he was moving closer. The kiss started out light and gentle, just as it had the night before. With mouths meeting. Breath mingling. Passion still leashed, but straining to break free.

And no wonder. One taste of the woman wasn't enough. Not by a long shot. He angled his head, delving deeper and giving himself over to need. She didn't seem to mind. In fact, she kept up with him just fine. Her hands had gone from trapped safely between their bodies to his shoulders and now were fisted in his hair, letting him know he wasn't the only one being carried away.

Stop!

His silent command went unheeded. Thomas wanted more and, gauging from her response, so did Elizabeth. It was mutual, consensual. Briefly, he considered his options. Her bedroom was just down the hall, but occupied at the moment with one very large and overprotective dog that Thomas could hear whining for freedom even over the blood rushing in his ears. The love seat was closer anyway. He backed toward it and lowered himself onto the curved arm. They could work their way around to the cushions in a minute. Right now, he preferred Elizabeth right where she was, standing between the *V* of his legs with her small, perfect breasts nearly level with his mouth.

Her hair was mussed from his fingers. Her lips full and inviting. Her gaze was wide. Expectant? Eager?

Go slow.

This silent command was easier to follow than the last one. He brought his mouth to her neck, nipping softly with his teeth as he worked his way lower. Elizabeth tilted her head to the side and he continued down. At her collarbone, he stopped, savored, even as the buttons on her blouse beckoned.

As his eager fingers fumbled with the top one, her breath sighed out as if she were luxuriating in the moment. Meanwhile, his pulse had picked up speed and the breath sawed from his lungs, hot and urgent.

Thomas was two buttons in when she decided to return the favor. Her fingers were much more nimble than his and made fast work of the buttons holding his shirt together. When she finished, she pushed it back onto his shoulders. The corners of that sexy mouth curved up. There was no mistaking the desire in her dark eyes. No mistaking it at all.

Curiously, it helped stopped him from doing something foolish. He couldn't do this. *They* couldn't do this. Sex would complicate things. No doubt, Elizabeth would read too much into the act, especially given the current role-playing that was going on. Physical need would turn into emotional need. She would expect more than he was able to give. It was best to nip this in the bud before she got hurt, Thomas decided, refusing to consider that the heart he was hoping to protect from harm very well might be his own.

He pulled his shirt back over his shoulders.

"This got a little out of hand, I'm afraid. I only meant to kiss you like I did last night. Sorry."

Elizabeth stumbled back a couple steps, looking as if she'd been slapped. He regretted that, but it was better this way. For both of them. He needed her to *act* as if she loved him. Not to actually fall for him.

She reworked the buttons on her blouse,

fastening them all the way to the throat. He hadn't gotten a chance to see what was beneath the fabric, except for a tantalizing glimpse of pink lace. That, along with her wounded expression, would keep him awake tonight.

"We need to get used to doing that," he managed to say in a matter-of-fact tone. It was a pitiful explanation for his behavior, but she nodded anyway.

He rose and buttoned his own shirt. Instead of tucking the tails into his trousers once again, he left them out as a cover for his arousal. He was nearly to the door when she stopped him with one quietly issued question.

"Do you think we will?"

He turned, studied her. The woman had him stirred up on so many levels. In the span of a couple dates that weren't really dates at all, she had him sharing things and remembering things and, worst of all, wanting things that he'd long ago decided were off the table when it came to negotiating the terms of his future happiness.

And so it was that, just before he rushed out her door, he said with great feeling, "God, I hope so."

CHAPTER EIGHT

ELIZABETH woke the following morning with a headache that throbbed long after she'd downed a couple of painkillers with her first cup of coffee.

It didn't help that Howie and the pesky squirrel started their game of chase as soon as she opened the front door. Already, her neighbor from across the street had come calling. Mrs. Hildabrand had stood on Elizabeth's porch, decked out in curlers and a worn plaid robe, complaining and threatening to make another nuisance report.

All that before seven o'clock and a second cup of coffee.

Elizabeth was sipping that second cup now while sitting in her quiet kitchen. Howie, suitably chastised, sprawled on the rug in front of the sink. She swore he was pouting. With the mug cupped in both hands, she sat on the chair Thomas had occupied the evening before. His herringbone jacket remained draped over the back of it. Though he'd returned for it, he'd still wound up forgetting it.

But he hadn't forgotten to kiss her…and then some.

A sloppy mix of emotions churned inside of her at the memory. Curiously, embarrassment over her enthusiastic response wasn't among them. Perhaps she would be embarrassed the next time she saw him, but right now she was still tingling all over and regretting that he'd stopped.

She tilted her head to one side and, when she caught the scent of his cologne, inhaled deeply. Potent stuff, that. It suited him. Everything about the man packed a punch. Just as every time she thought she had him figured out, he threw her for a loop. He'd come on to her last night like a man who was very much interested in more than a business deal or friendship. Then he'd stopped. He'd *apologized*!

She was still struggling to make sense of his parting words in response to her foolishly uttered question about whether or not they would ever get used to kissing one another.

God, I hope so!

He'd said it so emphatically, but what exactly did he mean? And why did the possibilities leave her both excited and leery? A glance at the clock reminded her she didn't have time to figure it out now.

After showering, she stood clad in a towel and rummaged through her closet for something to wear to the office, dismissing one outfit after another until she'd worked her way through her entire wardrobe. Maybe Mel was right about her needing some new clothes. Eyeing the panorama of outfits, it struck Elizabeth that practically every article of clothing in her closet came in one of four colors: black, white, navy or tan. A bland and boring palate that also was abundantly safe. She didn't need to worry about drawing attention to herself, whether negative or positive, garbed in these things. No one really noticed her, and that had suited Elizabeth just fine after growing up with her "out-there" parents.

She certainly hadn't learned anything about fashion from her mother, except what to avoid. Delphine sewed her own clothes and accessories from colorful scraps of old fabric. Sometimes she even tried to sell her creations at local craft shows. She didn't have many takers. The outfits were creative and economical, but hardly stylish. Even so, Delphine loved the attention her homemade clothes attracted—and they attracted plenty.

At first, holey blue jeans were patched in bold hues. Later, her mother recycled them into skirts, shorts and even purses. That wasn't so bad, but polka-dotted bedsheets or mattress ticking turned up as tunics, bandanas and skirts. The winter Elizabeth turned thirteen her mother had turned green wool blankets from an army surplus store into long, shapeless coats for the entire family. It was impossible not to stand out while wearing pea-green bedding, which was why she'd started buying her own clothes as soon as she was able to squirrel away funds from a regular babysitting gig. That is, what the family didn't require to keep a roof over their heads.

Pushing wet hair back from her face now, Elizabeth eyed her reflection in the full-length mirror. She'd gone from one extreme to the other, from standing out to blending in, but there was no help for it now. Besides, why should it matter to her? It didn't matter to Thomas. Indeed, he'd picked her for the role of his make-believe fiancée based on her appearance alone. She looked like a "Beth," or she had. And she'd been in the right place at the right time.

She would do well to remember that, despite his later claims about no longer judging a book by its cover.

Chin lifted in annoyance with herself as much as defiance, Elizabeth reached back into the closet and chose her oldest, most conservative black suit—the one Mel had dubbed Abbey-wear, because she claimed Elizabeth looked as if she was headed for a nunnery whenever she wore it.

She was slipping into her most comfortable pair of shoes—a low-heeled design in scuffed black—when her cell phone jangled. She glanced at the small screen. Despite her best efforts, her pulse went all wonky upon seeing the caller's identity.

"Hello, Thomas."

"Hi. Good morning. I hope I'm not catching you at a bad time."

"Not at all. I'm just getting ready to leave for the office." She gave herself a mental high five for managing to sound perfectly nonchalant and normal despite the kicked-up cadence of her pulse.

"Same here."

"Are you calling about your jacket?" she asked. It was the reason they'd gone back inside her house last night.

"My…ah, right. My jacket. I left it in your kitchen, didn't I?"

"Yes. I saw it on the back of the chair this morning." And then she'd sat there sniffing his cologne like an idiot. "I'll return it when we see each other again, unless you think you'll need it sooner."

"No. But that's what I'm calling about. I realized after I left your place last night that we never decided when we would meet today."

Probably because they'd both had other things on their minds. *Business, business, business,* Elizabeth reminded herself now when her barely settled pulse got all wonky again. Forcing her focus to her schedule, she said in her most professional tone, "I've got a meeting at ten o'clock that I can't reschedule. After that, though, I can shuffle a couple meetings around if you want to have lunch together."

Lunch was safe as long as it was in a populated place where public displays of affection would be inappropriate, assuming he had any such displays in mind.

"Unfortunately, I'm busy from eleven-thirty until nearly four going over the results of a marketing survey." He waited only a beat before saying, "How about dinner again?"

"Dinner?"

"Or we could meet up later in the evening if you've got something going on."

"No. Dinner's better. There's an Indian restaurant not far from the campus that I've been wanting to try. How does that sound?"

"Good. And spicy. Just like you like it." Had she imagined that strangled tone?

"I'll meet you there at—"

"No. I'll come by and pick you up."

"Oh, that's not necessary." Indeed, until she got her feelings under control, it bordered on cruel and usual punishment.

"If this is about last night—"

"It's not," she lied.

"Still, I feel I should apologize again for… what happened."

What did it say about her, Elizabeth wondered, that she would much rather he apologized for what *hadn't*?

"Don't! I mean, there's really no need. As you said last night, we both just got a little carried away." Not nearly far enough that she'd woken up feeling boneless and satisfied, but enough that his obvious regrets now were starting to make her feel like a first-class idiot.

"Yes. We did." He was quiet a moment. His tone was oddly resolute when he said, "I'll pick you up. Just tell me what time."

"Does five-thirty sound okay?" Arguing would only make her seem more foolish, she decided. It would make it seem as if she didn't trust herself to be alone with him. In a car. For a short drive. To a restaurant. For spicy food.

"Sure. Five-thirty."

"At my office," she added hastily. "I'll be out front at five-fifteen."

She trusted herself, but still…

"What's with the Abbey-wear?" Mel wanted to know even before Elizabeth had a chance to boot up her computer. "I thought we agreed that you would burn that overly conservative getup and donate the shoes to an old folks home."

"It's comfortable." Elizabeth sniffed.

"Comfort can be attractive, hon."

Her friend should know. Mel looked perfectly at ease strutting around in a pair of stilettos. Today, the stilettos were a bright raspberry color and she'd paired them with a navy suit that might have been considered conservative if not for the high slit in the skirt and Mel's well-defined curves.

She looked gorgeous, of course. And stylish. Standing near her, Elizabeth felt especially frumpy. She was one hundred and eighty degrees the opposite of Delphine and her cacophony of colors all right. Unfortunately, that still didn't make Elizabeth's wardrobe choices any more fashionable.

Her irritation came out in the form of defiance.

"I'm not going to change my appearance and contort myself to fit into someone else's ideal of beauty, especially when he probably wouldn't care anyway."

"Okaaaay." Mel pursed her lips. "I was going to ask how last night went, but I think I have my answer. I take it Thomas wants you to dress differently and you're rebelling by wearing your, um, least flattering attire."

Frowning, Elizabeth replied, "This suit isn't that bad. It's a high quality label, I'll have you know. It didn't come cheaply."

"Then in addition to committing a fashion crime, you were robbed," Mel remarked blandly.

Elizabeth let it drop since the price tag really was a moot point. Instead, she plucked at the jacket's prim mandarin collar, determined not to recall the way Thomas had fumbled with the buttons on her blouse the previous night, and said, "Actually, this is how his Beth would dress."

"*His* Beth?"

"You know what I mean, Mel. That's his fiancée's name as far as his grandmother is aware. I'm just the stand-in for the girl of his…"

"Dreams?"

"More like imagination."

"So, in order for you to be plausible as *his Beth*, he's encouraging you to play down your best assets."

"No. Thomas has never said anything one way or another about the way I dress." Elizabeth frowned again. "Although, last night after dinner, he did remove the headband I was wearing."

He'd seemed agitated at the time. Frustrated?

"Is that all he removed?" Mel bobbed her eyebrows twice.

Another time, Elizabeth would have laughed. Mel was good at that. Her knack for levity had served them both well over the years, and it never failed to put their clients at ease. But her words had Elizabeth recalling the shirt she'd been helping Thomas remove.

"Nothing happened."

"Nothing?" Mel crossed her arms.

Sighing, Elizabeth slumped down onto the seat of her chair. "Nothing *much*. He…kissed me again."

"And you liked it. Again," Mel surmised. "Face it. You like *him*."

Some of Elizabeth's annoyance with herself

and Thomas leaked away. Frustration and a fresh dollop of confusion took its place.

"What's not to like?" She sighed in defeat.

Her friend levered a hip onto Elizabeth's desk. "Are we talking about the kiss in this case or the man responsible for it?"

"Either. Both."

"Uh-oh."

"There's no 'uh-oh,' Mel. There can be no 'uh-oh.' Thomas is a nice guy, and he's very likeable."

"Don't forget hot," Mel inserted on a wink.

"No need to remind me on that score." But now that she had, Elizabeth's internal thermostat was working its way into the red. "The man sure knows how to kiss. But we're *not* dating."

She said the last part a little too emphatically. Mel's eyes narrowed. "I gather you're having a bit of trouble remembering that."

"Guilty as charged. I wasn't expecting—"

"Fireworks," Mel finished.

Oh, yeah. And a dizzying display, no less. But since mention of their sexual chemistry was too damning to dwell on, Elizabeth said, "Actually, I wasn't expecting us to have much, if anything, in common."

"But you do."

"We both like Hitchcock movies and spicy

Chinese." She chuckled at the memory of Thomas fumbling his food during dinner. "Even if he can't use chopsticks to save his life." Her grin was short-lived. "God, Mel. He's exactly the kind of man a smart woman steers clear of."

"But you have common interests, and I thought you just said he was nice and likeable and hot?"

"We do and he's nice and likeable and hot, all right. He's also smart and sexy, and…from what I can tell, the flattering adjectives are practically endless where Thomas is concerned." She grabbed Mel's arm. "Did I tell you about his manners? He pulls out chairs, opens doors. He even apologizes when he swears, not that he makes a habit of it."

"Apologizing?"

"Swearing." She let go of her friend's arm.

Mel shook her head. "I'm sorry, hon. I'm not seeing the problem here. You obviously like him. I *know* you like the way he kisses. And he likes you."

Elizabeth closed her eyes briefly and took a deep breath.

"No, Mel. Thomas *needs* me. That's one of the big red flags waving madly here. This is business."

The corners of Mel's mouth turned down

in dismissal and she shook her head. "I'm not buying that. He *likes* you, and as more than a pal," her friend insisted again. "You've already agreed to spend some time with him *acting* like a happy couple. So what if a little pleasure is starting to slip into your business arrangement? What will it hurt? For that matter, who knows where it will lead?"

"I know where it will lead. Nowhere."

But Mel shook her head again. "You are one of the smartest, most self-assured women I've ever met when you're dealing in a professional capacity. But you don't give yourself enough credit where men are concerned. He may just fall gorgeous head over pricey wing tips for you, for real."

No wonky pulse now. Instead, Elizabeth's stomach took a roller-coaster-worthy plunge. Is that what she wanted to happen? She wasn't sure. They didn't know one another well enough. Yet. Even if everything she knew about him so far, she liked. Except… "He's anti-commitment," she told Mel.

"Come on. Did he actually say that?"

"Yep." Elizabeth nodded. "He made it clear in no uncertain terms when we had dinner the first night that he has no plans to settle down. Ever."

"All men say that."

"No. He means it." Her heart squeezed as she relayed what Thomas had told her the previous night about his parents, the horrifying car accident that had claimed his mother and his father's subsequent alcoholism. "He thinks of love as a disease, a chronic one is how he phrased it."

Mel nibbled the inside of her cheek, uncharacteristically quiet. At last she said, "In his defense, he had a tough break. He was a kid when the accident happened and so it was easy for him to see love as the reason his father is the way he is. But that doesn't make it so. His father suffers from a disease all right. Alcoholism. That's why he basically abandoned his son. The accident might have been the trigger, but…" She lifted her shoulders. "The poor guy. It's no wonder he turned out so gun-shy."

"I know." Elizabeth sighed again. "I wish he could be just a jerk, though. You know?"

"Yeah. A garden variety misogynist would make your situation less complicated," Mel agreed. "You could always tell him that you've reconsidered your bargain and want out. We can find another way to make Literacy Liaisons's endowment a reality."

"I've thought about that, but I've committed myself." Ironic laughter followed her statement. "At least one of us is capable of doing so."

"Are you sure you want to go through with this?"

Elizabeth hesitated only a moment. "I'm sure. It's only for a matter of days. This time next week, Thomas and I will have gone our separate ways."

Yet that thought brought precious little in the way of comfort, a fact Elizabeth tried to ignore.

"Well, at least your eyes are wide open," Mel said.

"Yep. Wide open. There's no changing someone who doesn't want to change. You can push and prod and you just wind up shoving them further away."

"Are you okay?"

"Sure. I like Thomas, and I'm definitely attracted to him, but it's not as if I'm in love with him or anything," she hastened to assure them both. "Right now, I've got paperwork to catch up on." She swiveled in her seat and began typing her password as Mel started for the door.

"Elizabeth?"

"Hmm." She glanced up from her computer screen in time to catch Mel's worried frown.

"Your eyes, I know you said they're wide

open, but prop them that way with toothpicks, 'kay?"

In lieu of toothpicks, Elizabeth got down to business. Personal business. There would be no meandering conversation during dinner tonight, she decided. That was too much like what occurred on real dates. Nope. She would treat this like a job interview even though, technically, she'd already been hired. She created a file and made a list of questions she needed answered. Then she spent the next fifteen minutes ruminating over what more to tell him about herself.

She decided to break the information down into likes and dislikes. Since he already knew her preferences when it came to movie genres, directors and actors, she started with music, moved on to authors and completed the entertainment category with board games, adding in the dislike category her disdain for the computer variety.

From there she moved on to her basic values, causes beyond literacy that she supported and a very brief sketch of her education, since he already knew she'd attended State. She considered attaching her high school and college transcripts, but that seemed overkill.

As for her childhood, Thomas had met

Howie and she knew that as a child he'd owned a cockatiel named Hitchcock. She jotted down the names of the guinea pig, flop-eared rabbit and pair of very long-lived gold-fish she'd had while growing up.

When it came to her parents, she filled in their vital stats, leaving out their lack of a marriage certificate and their other free-spir-ited oddities. As for her brother, she touched on Ross only briefly, in part because she knew so little about him these days, including his whereabouts.

She swallowed thickly and touched his name on the computer screen. She missed him. As always, she wondered if he ever would decide to come home. Unlike her par-ents, she did not view her brother's vagabond lifestyle as freedom even if it was a kind of escape. No, Ross had run away. It didn't matter that he'd been five months shy of eigh-teen years old at the time, close enough to adulthood, according to their parents, to make his own choices.

"He's happy," Delphine had claimed at the time. "You like school and you were smart enough to get a scholarship. But not every-one's cut out for book-learning and college, Lizzie."

Skeet had seconded the opinion. And why

not? Their father had gotten by on charm and luck, working odd jobs to raise his family. More often than not he'd been paid under the table. If at times they'd had to live with relatives or crash in friends' apartments that was okay in his book.

It's all good. That was Skeet and Delphine's mantra.

But they weren't to blame for Ross's leaving. No that fell squarely on Elizabeth's shoulders. Where their folks hadn't been tough enough on Ross, Elizabeth had been unyielding in her nagging after he quit school.

"You're squandering your life," she'd raged during that final argument before he'd left home for good. "You're going to end up penniless, homeless."

"Mom and Dad have done just fine."

"That depends on your definition of fine, Ross. How many times would we have wound up in a shelter if not for friends or family opening their homes to us? In the meantime, the job market has only gotten more competitive."

"You're competitive enough for all of us." He hadn't intended it as a compliment. "When are you going to accept that I'm not smart like you?"

He was smart, every bit as bright as she

was. Intelligence and literacy didn't go hand-in-hand. But she'd nicked his pride and had put him on the defensive, a mistake she never made these days with Literacy Liaisons's clients.

If she hadn't been so critical of Ross, so self-righteous and pushy, he would have been comfortable confiding in her what their parents had long known. Ross could barely read above a third-grade level. Instead, he'd bolted without speaking another word to her.

Thomas thought her cause noble. He thought she was so selfless in starting up her nonprofit and wanting to see it survive. Indeed, last night he'd told her she was perfect.

Elizabeth knew the truth. She was anything but.

After that steamy encounter in her living room, Thomas worried that he would have a hard time keeping his hands to himself the next time he saw Elizabeth.

He worried that once again he would be compelled to satisfy his curiosity where she was concerned. And that was all this was, he assured himself, a really severe case of curiosity.

What else could it be?

Of course he liked her. It was impossible not to. She was smart, ambitious, interesting and all of that. A little voice in the back of his mind kept reminding him that brains and spunk had never proved such a huge turn-on in the past. Nor had he ever found himself this wildly attracted to a woman he would describe as cute and petite.

And then there was that tantalizing glimpse of pink lace he'd spied beneath her blouse. The memory of it was eating away at his peace of mind. Like a rip in the paper wrapping on a Christmas present, it invited his imagination to fill in the blanks. And was it ever.

Even so, he would make sure everything between them returned to normal—or as normal as possible given the odd set of circumstances surrounding their relationship.

They didn't.

The first indication came that evening almost immediately after he picked her up for dinner.

"This is for you," she said. They were stopped at a red light when she presented him with what amounted to a resume that included her background and interests.

"Ah, this is…helpful." The light turned green and he pulled ahead, not sure what else to say.

"I thought it would be. Time being so tight and all." He barely had a chance to digest that when she told him, "I made a questionnaire for you to fill out."

"A questionnaire."

"You don't need to fill it out tonight. You can get it back to me later. By tomorrow afternoon, say. I included my fax number at the top of the first page."

"Fax," he repeated inanely.

"Yes. I thought this would be a time-saver. Of course, you can email it to me if you'd prefer. My office email address is on the business card I gave you."

He wanted to appreciate her professional approach to the matter, but he'd been enjoying the way they had been going about getting to know one another.

They arrived at the restaurant and Thomas handed the keys to the valet. Elizabeth was out of the car and almost to the door before he caught up with her. For a small woman, she moved fast and with just enough sway to her hips to make up for the severe cut of her suit.

Was she wearing anything pink and lacy underneath it today? That question, inappropriate though it might be, occupied his thoughts through the salad course, and had his gaze straying time and again to the prim mandarin collar. He imagined himself unfastening the top button, albeit with a bit more finesse than he'd exhibited the previous night, and then working his way down.

He reached for his ice water and downed half the glass before setting it back on the table.

"So, tell me about your day?" He worked up a smile. "Any success stories to share?"

He'd asked the question as much to break the silence as to redirect his thoughts. Whatever his motives, though, he was rewarded with a smile.

"One of our clients read *Mr. Brown Can Moo! Can You?* today. Aloud. Cover to cover. Dr. Seuss in case you're wondering."

"My mom used to read it to me. It was one of my favorites as a kid." He smiled, surprised by the happy memory. He'd locked away so much of his pre-accident childhood that the good had been banished along with the bad.

"Mine, too. Anyway, our client got through the entire story with no mistakes. And there wasn't a dry eye in the room afterward." Elizabeth's eyes grew bright now at the recollection. "He's thirty-four, has twin toddler daughters and when he first came to see us more than a year ago his goal was to be able to read them a bedtime story."

"Now he can. That's nice. For him and for you." He reached into his pocket, pulled out his handkerchief and handed it to her. "Your job must be very satisfying."

"It is." She sipped the diet cola she'd ordered. "What about you? What did you do today?"

"Nothing quite as rewarding as hearing someone read their first book." He shrugged. "Mostly I shuffled through paperwork with Waverly's chief financial officer. We had plans for an expansion, but they've had to be put on hold. Some of our financing fell through. Now, we're busy trying to line up some other investors."

"That can't be easy in this economy."

"About as easy as reaching your endowment fund's goal."

"You're making that possible."

Though she smiled after she said it, the warmth of a moment earlier was gone. She returned to business mode and, before long, had him hauling out the form she'd filled out. Before the waiter came to ask if they wanted dessert, Thomas had a bad case of indigestion, but he knew that Elizabeth had once owned a guinea pig named Ziggy, a floppy-eared bunny named Kip and a pair of goldfish she'd called Bonnie and Clyde.

How was it possible, Thomas wondered, that even though he knew a lot more about her, he found her more of a puzzle than before?

After they finished their meal, he drove her back to her car in Literacy Liaisons's parking lot. The ride had been nerve-gratingly quiet. Now, as he stood next to her car after opening the door for her, the mood progressed from strained to outright awkward.

"Good night." He leaned in to kiss her, intending a quick, chaste and perfunctory peck, but she stuck out her hand instead. It poked him just below his breastbone.

"Sorry." She coughed. "I know you said we should get used to kissing and pretending to be affectionate with one another, but I'm really not comfortable doing that."

This came as a surprise, and not necessarily a good one. Here he'd been steeling himself for physical contact, determined not to let a simple kiss boil out of control, and she was essentially telling him thanks, but no seconds for me. He'd never had a complaint when it came to his kissing and Elizabeth hadn't seemed to mind it the previous night. In fact, she'd participated rather enthusiastically, if memory served correctly. His ego had Thomas pointing that out.

"You seemed pretty comfortable last night."

"Yes, well, I think it blurs the lines a little too much given the true nature of our relationship."

"Uh-huh."

She swallowed and he needed to believe her expression held some regret before she added, "But don't worry, Thomas. When we're around your grandmother, I won't pull away if you put your arm around me or anything."

"Gee, that's good to know."

"As for the rest, if she asks, maybe you could just tell her that Beth isn't comfortable with public displays of affection."

He didn't remind her that he no longer thought she look like a Beth. The name was beside the point. She'd referred to herself in the third person. If that didn't imply distance, Thomas didn't know what did. What could he do but respect her wishes? He shook her hand, bid her good-night. Just before she slipped into the car, he told her, "I'll have that questionnaire filled out and faxed over first thing in the morning."

By the time Thomas arrived home twenty minutes later, he was feeling particularly cranky. The house, a large ranch-style on a cul-de-sac in a newer subdivision populated with professionals, was quiet. Though the evening air was hot and humid, he turned off the air-conditioning and opened the windows. The sound of crickets, however, did little to ease his agitation. Nor did filling out Elizabeth's questionnaire.

His inseam and sleeve length? Really? Thomas might have found her attention to detail amusing if not for the fact that he had dozens of questions when it came to the woman, and not one of them focused on her clothing sizes.

Two hours later, he was pacing his bedroom when the telephone on the nightstand rang.

"Tommy, hello," Nana Jo greeted him when he answered. "I wasn't sure I would catch you at home."

A glance at the clock showed it was after ten. Worry came instantly, as it always did where his grandmother was concerned. "Is everything okay?"

"Fine. Just getting excited about the weekend."

"I am, too." It was the truth, for the most part. He always looked forward to seeing his grandmother.

"I can't wait to meet Beth. You're both still coming, right?"

"On Friday, yes." He pushed aside his nerves. "In fact, she and I talked about the weekend over dinner tonight." He had to admit, it felt really good not to have to lie to his grandmother, even if he still wasn't being completely truthful.

He heard the smile in her voice when Nana Jo asked, "Did you take her to a fancy restaurant with candlelit tables and strolling violinists?"

"I don't know that they have those anyplace but in old movies," he replied. "We ate at an Indian restaurant. It was more comfortable than fancy, but our table did have a candle on it." He recalled the way the flame had reflected in Elizabeth's dark eyes. "It was nice."

"An Indian restaurant. I've never been to one. It sounds exotic and spicy."

Thomas smiled at Nana Jo's assessment. "Elizabeth has an adventurous palate."

"Is she with you now?"

"Nana Jo, she's not that kind of girl," he said on a laugh that only served to mock his libido. "Besides, we both have to work in the morning."

"I know how young people are now. I'm just pleased you decided to get married rather than move in together. That seems to be what everyone does nowadays. But when it's right and you're in love, why not make it legally binding?"

Because Thomas found what his grand-mother was saying to make way too much sense, he decided to end the conversation.

Thomas figured he would see Elizabeth again before the weekend, but it didn't happen. They spoke by telephone a couple of times, and she'd emailed him once to let him know that she'd received his fax. Other than that, nothing.

He had to admit that he was disappointed, especially when she turned down his offer to see a Hitchcock film at the restored Michigan Theater on Thursday night. He'd been sure she would jump at the chance. Indeed, he'd thought of her the moment he'd spied the marquee announcing performance times for *Vertigo* while driving down East Liberty.

He'd been thinking of her a lot, regardless of—or perhaps because of—the way she'd insisted on shaking his hand when they parted on Wednesday night. But no more face-to-face meetings occurred, let alone sequels to that heated encounter in her living room that still ran through his mind in a never-ending loop.

If Elizabeth were another woman, he might think she was playing hard to get. He didn't like the fact that if she were another woman it wouldn't be working.

Thomas was eager to see her again, a fact that had him nervous as he packed his bag for the long weekend early Friday morning. His trepidation increased tenfold when he arrived at her home to collect her just after nine and she met him at the door with no suitcase in sight.

"I appreciate a woman who packs light, but don't you think you'll need a few things?" he asked.

She tucked her hands into the back pockets of a pair of khaki capris. "I was thinking we could just go for the day instead of for the entire weekend."

"The day? My grandmother lives in Charlevoix, Elizabeth." The city was located on the northwest side of the Lower Peninsula, a good four-hour drive from Ann Arbor even without the added holiday traffic they were likely to encounter despite getting a jump on the weekend.

"I realize that, but the less time we spend with her, the fewer questions she'll be able to ask. I'll share the driving," she offered, as if to sweeten the deal.

"Nana Jo is going to have questions either way and, believe me, she won't hesitate to ask them, whether in person or over the telephone." Of course, then answering them would be his problem to deal with rather than hers.

"Do you talk on the phone often?"

"Pretty much every day, but I haven't seen her in months. I miss her."

He hadn't intended to use the sentiment to score points, but Elizabeth softened. He saw it in her expression.

"Tell you what," he began. "We can come home on Sunday instead of Monday. You mentioned before that you'd canceled some of your plans to accompany me. Maybe the weekend won't be a total bust for you if we leave a day early."

"I was just going to go to the beach with Mel and some other girlfriends." She shrugged. "It was no big deal."

"Don't you do anything with your family?"

"My parents have an annual barbecue on the Fourth."

She hadn't told him much about them, and even the written biography she'd given him the other evening contained precious little information beyond their names and dates of birth, so he was intrigued. "Good. Then you will be able to attend it. Will your brother be there? Ross, right?"

She shook her head. He'd said something wrong, something that made her sad, though he wasn't sure what. But then, he knew better than most people that sometimes innocent questions about family could be as wounding as daggers. Hoping to chase the shadows from her eyes, he said, "There's nothing like a good barbecue to celebrate Independence Day."

He was relieved when Elizabeth's smile reappeared. "You don't know my parents," she said wryly.

No. Thomas didn't. He'd always made it a point not to meet the parents of any of the women he spent time with. He didn't worry about passing parental inspection. Rather, he knew the signal it would send to the other party. Meeting the parents made even the most casual relationship seem serious, at least where the marriage-minded were concerned.

Oddly, he found himself wanting to meet Elizabeth's, even—or maybe especially—after she asked, "Have you ever had tofu shish kebabs?"

"I can't say that I have."

"It's an acquired taste, believe me. The same can be said for soy-and-kelp burgers on unleavened bread."

"Soy and kelp, huh?" He rubbed the back of his neck. "I hope you're not too bored with

Nana Jo's tame cooking. I think the most exotic recipe in her repertoire is fried green tomatoes. She started making them after she saw the movie of the same name."

"I'm nothing like my parents," she replied hastily, giving Thomas the impression that, just as he was, she was eager to ensure that the apple fell far from the tree and then kept right on rolling.

Elizabeth invited him inside while she packed her bag. Howie wasn't there. Mel had taken him back to her town house. If the dog were there, Thomas had little doubt it would be growling menacingly. It was if the hound knew that something about his owner's relationship with Thomas wasn't all it seemed to be.

Thomas paced the living room. His gaze kept straying to the love seat, specifically to the arm where he'd sat the other evening while he and Elizabeth had eagerly started helping one another out of their clothes. Sanity had prevailed, but he'd been going crazy ever since. After fifteen of the longest minutes of his life, Elizabeth finally emerged with a small carry-on-sized suitcase in hand.

"You really do pack light."

She shrugged. "A couple pairs of walking shorts, two shirts and nightclothes don't take up much room. You didn't specify a dress code."

She sounded defiant.

"There isn't one. My grandmother is pretty laid-back." He pointed toward the bag. "A bathing suit might come in handy. There's a nice stretch of beach nearby."

Elizabeth shook her head. "I burn easily."

And blushed easily, too, he noted.

"Well, I brought mine, but suit yourself." He took her bag. "Ready?"

In answer, she started for the front door, which she carefully locked behind them. Then they were on their way, heading toward the interstate in his car as Bruce Springsteen belted out "Born in the U.S.A." on the radio.

For better or for worse, there was no turning back now.

CHAPTER NINE

ELIZABETH hadn't intended to fall asleep, but a little over two hours into their trip she dozed off. Before then she and Thomas hadn't spoken much, other than to comment on the good weather—forecasters were calling for sunshine and warm temperatures through the early part of the following week—and go over a few details of the visit.

She missed their easy conversation, but keeping things all business was for the best. The lines of their relationship weren't likely to become too blurry that way. So, she'd pulled out a magazine she'd brought with her and made a point of reading it. Or, rather, pretending to read it. Now that she was awake, she couldn't recall a single article.

She straightened in her seat and stretched before sending a sheepish smile Thomas's way.

"Sorry about that. I guess I drifted off."

"That's all right. You only snored a little."

He winked after saying so. She could only hope he was kidding.

"Where are we?"

"About fifteen minutes south of Charlevoix. I thought we'd visit with my grandmother a bit before checking in at the bed-and-breakfast where we'll be staying."

In separate rooms. He'd made that clear after she'd made a point of asking him about it via email. Still, they would be under the same roof and that was enough to have her nerves and newfound needs percolating on high.

Elizabeth had never been to Charlevoix. Though her family had moved around a lot during her childhood, they'd done so mainly in the much more populated southern part of the state. So, she stared out the window as they made their way down Bridge Street with its quaint assortment of shops and eateries, acting the part of the tourist. Thomas indulged her, pointing out a fudge shop and other sights of interest, and giving her some background. The vast expanse of Lake Michigan stretched to the west of the town. The much smaller Lake Charlevoix was to the east.

"It's pretty here."

"It is. Nana Jo likes it, even though the winters can be harsh."

"She stays here year-round?"

"Yes." He chuckled then. "She's quite adamant that she'll never become one of those snowbirds who flies to Florida before the first snowflake falls. She and my late grandfather had always planned to retire here. He died when I was six. Heart attack. She was still set on moving to Charlevoix eventually. She was already looking at places at the time of the accident. Then she put everything on hold."

For him.

"Sorry about your grandfather," Elizabeth murmured. Josephine O'Keefe had lost her husband and only child in the span of two years. It wasn't only pity Elizabeth felt for the other woman, but admiration. She'd rolled up her sleeves and put her own plans on hold to raise a young, equally grief-stricken boy. "Your grandmother sounds like an amazing woman."

Thomas glanced over. His hand left the steering wheel to give hers a gentle squeeze. "She is. You're going to like her."

Elizabeth didn't need his reassurance. She already did, and it was a realization that made her all the more uneasy.

Nana Jo lived in a condominium complex not far from downtown, but only a short distance from the lake.

"Well, this is it," Thomas said, pulling

into the parking lot. He sounded every bit as nervous as Elizabeth felt when he asked, "Ready?"

"As I'm ever going to be," she murmured.

She opened the car door before he had a chance to come around and do it for her, earning a frown. The day was warm, a fact the automobile's air-conditioning had done a good job of camouflaging. The sun's heat would have been unbearable if not for the stiff breeze blowing in off the lakes. It snatched at her neatly ordered hair and sent it flying around her face.

It also brought with it the appealing scents of summer, including the smoke from someone's barbecue. Before she'd dozed off, Thomas had asked if she wanted to stop for a bite to eat. She'd told him no, that she wasn't hungry. At the time she hadn't been. Nerves had tied her stomach into knots and she had been eager to get to their final destination. Now, her stomach growled and she found herself wishing for the last-minute reprieve of a meal.

Before she could say so to Thomas, however, she heard a squeal of delight. She turned to see a stylish older woman with a short cap of silver hair bustling across the parking lot toward them with her smile stretching nearly as wide as her arms.

"Tommy!"

He hugged the woman back, picking her up off her feet in the process. Elizabeth smiled as she watched them and something inside of her shifted to boggy ground once again. What was it Mel always said? You can judge how a man will treat you by the way he treats his mother. Nana Jo wasn't Thomas's mother, but close enough that her friend's pearls of wisdom applied. God help her.

"It's good to see you, too," he managed to respond after a moment.

Raw emotion thickened his voice, leaving no doubt as to the deep love Thomas had for his grandmother, the deep love they had for one another. Tragedy had made their bond all the stronger. Elizabeth admired it. She admired them for the way they obviously cherished it.

Two expectant gazes focused on her then. Showtime, she thought, wishing wildly, before she could catch herself, that the moment could be real. That she could be the love of Thomas's life, brought home to meet the woman who'd raised him.

"And you're Tommy's Beth."

Even if Elizabeth had had time to stick out a hand in a gesture of greeting, it wouldn't have mattered. Nana Jo closed the distance between them in short order and pulled her into an embrace that, while not strong enough to break bones, thoroughly shattered Elizabeth's preconceptions of Josephine O'Keefe as a frail octogenarian nearing the end of her days.

"H-h-hi." The single syllable sputtered out along with Elizabeth's breath as the woman rocked her side to side.

"Nana Jo, stop. You'll crush her," Thomas chided lightly when the embrace lengthened.

His grandmother pulled back on a robust laugh. "I'm sorry, my dear. It's just that I'm so tickled to finally meet you. Tommy has told me so much about you."

She patted Elizabeth's cheek before grasping her lightly by the arms and taking a step back. Then she frowned.

"I have to admit, I pictured you a little differently."

"Different h-how?" Elizabeth cast a nervous glance toward Thomas. What sort of description had he given her?

"I don't know. Just…just thinking out loud and being insufferably rude," she apologized.

"That's not necessary. I can honestly say you're not quite how I pictured you, either." If Nana Jo's health was failing it sure didn't show.

"It's just that you're such a tiny thing,"

mused Nana Jo, who stood half a head taller and had a more substantial build. She smiled at Thomas. "The breeze coming off Lake Michigan will blow her away if you're not careful to keep a tight hold on her, Tommy."

"I plan to do just that."

His smile was as warm as the gaze he sent Elizabeth. Though the words were said for his grandmother's benefit, Elizabeth's breathing hitched and she smiled back.

Nana Jo grinned as well, before demanding of herself, "Goodness, where are my manners? You must think me a horrible hostess, Beth, waylaying you in the parking lot like this." She winked from behind a pair of red-rimmed bifocals. "I plead guilty to watching for your arrival from my windows and then hurrying down here the minute I spotted you, too eager to wait for you to ring the doorbell. Pop open the trunk of that fancy car of yours, Tommy. Let's get your bags and go inside where we can all sit down and have a proper visit. I just made a fresh pitcher of iced tea and some cookies."

Elizabeth could see where Thomas had learned his polite ways, but that wasn't what had her casting an urgent glance in his direction.

"I—I thought we were staying at a bed-and-breakfast in town, Thomas?"

"We are." Both his expression and tone were apologetic when he told his grandmother, "I've booked rooms for Elizabeth and I at the Daniels Cottage over on Edgewater, Nana."

"We didn't want to impose," Elizabeth explained.

Nana Jo made a *tsking* sound and waved one hand impatiently. "Impose? Nonsense! It's no imposition. Of course you'll stay here. I have plenty of space." To Thomas she said, "Beth will sleep in the guest room. I put fresh linens on the bed just this morning."

"Where will I be sleeping?" Thomas asked innocently. But Elizabeth thought she caught a dash of the devil in his otherwise angelic expression.

"On the couch," Nana Jo retorted. "I'm too old-fashioned to agree to let you sleep in the same room with Beth, whether she's your fiancée or not."

She winked again at Elizabeth, who felt her face catch fire.

"Really, that's very kind. But I...we couldn't put you out like that," Elizabeth began. "Besides, Thomas already made the reservations."

It was a weak argument that Nana Jo dismantled easily. "He can unmake them. If the owner gives you any trouble, Tommy, I'll talk to him. I know Ned and Estelle from church." Lowering her voice, she added, "Estelle is on the list to bring dessert for funeral lunches, but we never put her rum cake out. She's a little too liberal with the libations, if you know what I mean."

"But—"

"Not another word. I won't have it any other way. You're all but family now, my dear, and family is never a bother. Tell her, Tommy."

Before Elizabeth could object further, Thomas said, "Arguing won't do you any good, I'm afraid."

He put an arm around Elizabeth's shoulders. She jolted at his touch, but didn't pull away. She'd promised him that she wouldn't. She hadn't promised to snuggle closer, though. She did so automatically, reeled in by the scent of his cologne. When she felt him drop a light kiss on the top of her head, she came to her senses. It was all for show, she reminded herself, even if they were attracted to one another. Ultimately, nothing real and lasting would come of it.

"He comes by his stubborn streak honestly,

Beth. He gets it from me," Nana Jo claimed proudly. "Now let's see to your bags."

Thomas shrugged helplessly and mouthed an apology to Elizabeth. Even though they had decided to leave a day early, the weekend had just gotten much, much longer.

Nana Jo's condo was on the top floor. Despite their protests, she insisted on carrying Elizabeth's suitcase the entire time, not even setting it down during the short elevator ride. Thomas would have to have another chat with her doctor, he decided, and find out exactly what she should and shouldn't be doing. He knew better than to think he would get a straight answer from her. Stubborn streak, indeed. Hers was a mile wide.

Still, he was relieved to see her looking so healthy, not to mention so damned happy. She hadn't stopped grinning since their arrival. Thomas pushed away the twinge of guilt he felt for deceiving her. So far, the result was worth it.

She waved Elizabeth inside the condo, though she left it to Thomas to hold open the door. She patted his cheek on the way inside. The place was every bit as welcoming as she was, with the multitude of homey touches he remembered. Even though he hadn't grown up here, he'd spent enough time in the condo that he never felt like a guest.

Today, it smelled like a bakery thanks to a batch of fresh-from-the-oven cookies that were warming on the kitchen counter—chocolate chip, his favorite. He'd never brought home a woman before, but this was pretty much what he'd expected the reception to be. Nana Jo had pulled out all of the stops in an effort to make Elizabeth feel welcomed and comfortable. He eyed the couch sourly. Oh, yes. She'd thought of everything all right.

"If you want to freshen up, Beth, the guest bath is just down the hallway," Nana Jo was saying. "I've put out towels and a washcloth for you. If you need anything else or can't find something, don't hesitate to ask."

The grand tour didn't take long. Nana Jo's condo wasn't very large, even if it felt that way thanks to its open floor plan. In addition to two bedrooms and two full baths, it boasted an eat-in kitchen that was separated from the living room by a large, granite island.

He reached for one of the cookies on his way past, only to have his hand swatted away by Nana Jo, who barely glanced in his direction and never broke stride. The woman still had eyes in the back of her head.

"This is where you'll stay, Beth. Tommy,

you can leave your bag in here for now so that we're not tripping over it in the living room."

"Gee, how very generous of you," he grumbled good-naturedly.

"You haven't canceled your reservation at the bed-and-breakfast yet, if the accommodations here aren't to your liking," she reminded him tartly as one brow arched over the top rim of her bifocals. He could only chuckle, especially since Elizabeth was trying to tuck away a grin.

When they reached the guest room, he stopped at the door after the women continued inside. After setting his luggage in the corner, he leaned against the jamb and watched Elizabeth take in the inviting floral comforter that covered a queen-sized bed. Coordinating curtains flapped at the large, open window that let in a breeze that made air-conditioning obsolete even on a day as warm as this one.

"I'm sure I'll be very comfortable in here. The room is lovely, Mrs. O'Keefe."

"It's Nana Jo, dear. And thank you." His grandmother wagged a finger in his direction then. "Tommy complains that it's too feminine for his liking."

"I feel like I'm sleeping in a posey patch, but it suits you, Elizabeth." He managed to sound lighthearted, even though he was picturing her on the bed, surrounded by the comforter's fussy floral print and wearing nothing but a couple of scraps of pink lace. On a groan he spat out a mild oath.

"Tommy! Your language," Nana Jo admonished. "I raised you better than that. What on earth are you thinking?"

What was he thinking? He glanced at Elizabeth. Her eyes were wide, alert and, unless he missed his guess, full of interest. She moistened her lips, exhaled slowly. God help them both, *she* knew exactly what was on his mind.

While Elizabeth took his grandmother's suggestion and freshened up, Thomas helped Nana Jo carry out a tray of refreshments to the balcony that opened up off the living room. Large pots in the corners overflowed with bright red geraniums. Beyond the white wooden railing, Lake Michigan stretched as far as the eye could see. It was the kind of view one never tired of seeing. Even in the winter, when parts of the big lake froze and huge rafts of ice, pushed ashore by wind and waves, bounded the coast, the view was mesmerizing.

"It's a gorgeous day," he said.

"And yours is a gorgeous girl. I like your

Beth, Tommy." She poured three large glasses with iced tea and set a small plate of lemon wedges and a sugar bowl in the center of the scrolled iron table.

"I thought you would." He managed to purloin a cookie this time without getting his hand smacked.

"I still don't understand why it's taken you so long to finally bring her to see me." Her tone held reproach.

"I'm sorry I put you off for so long. Things were crazy at work and then, well, I just wanted to be sure." He'd told her similar things several times in the past. This time they seemed less like an excuse.

"And are you?"

The pat answer he planned never made it past his lips. Instead, he walked to the rail, his gaze trained on a couple of sailboats that were nothing but white dots on a cloudless blue horizon.

"I've never met anyone quite like Elizabeth," he said slowly, honestly. "I like being around her, spending time with her. The more I learn, the more I *want* to learn."

"You almost sound surprised."

"More like amazed." He took a bite of the cookie, turned and worked up a grin for her benefit. "She likes Alfred Hitchcock movies."

Nana Jo chuckled. "I see now what clinched the deal for you. That genre of film isn't for everyone."

"Actually, we have quite a bit in common, more than I expected."

"Well, that's what happens when you stop dating women who are all wrong for you."

He smiled since it was expected and finished the cookie, nearly choking on the last bite when his grandmother added, "Love has a way of finding us, Tommy. Even if we never look for it. Maybe especially when we don't."

Elizabeth joined them just as his coughing fit was subsiding. As soon as she stepped out onto the balcony, the breeze made a mockery of the time she'd spent returning her hair to its sleek bob. While she tucked it behind both ears, he rose from his seat and pulled out her chair, earning a nod of satisfaction from his grandmother.

"I'm so glad to finally have a chance to meet you, dear," Nana Jo said.

Just as he had, Elizabeth bypassed the sugar bowl and selected a wedge of lemon, which she squeezed into her glass.

"I'm enjoying meeting you, too. Thomas has told me a lot about you." Elizabeth smiled. "All of it good."

"Tommy, what have I told you about fibbing?" Nana Jo scolded, albeit teasingly.

Elizabeth looked uncomfortable despite her smile, but he had to hand it to her. She was managing to be completely honest with his grandmother despite the big white elephant of a lie sharing space with them on the small balcony.

"Tommy tells me you like Alfred Hitchcock."

"I do."

"And she plays poker, Nana Jo. She and some friends get together regularly." He sipped his tea. "No cigars but they sometimes talk sports."

"Really?" Nana Jo's eyes lit up. "I belong to a bridge club, but I always wanted to try my hand at five-card stud. Maybe you could teach me sometime?"

"Sure."

"You have to watch her, Elizabeth. My nana is a cardsharp."

They laughed and the conversation flowed freely until Nana Jo asked, "Why don't you tell me a little bit about your family? I haven't managed to get much out of Tommy on the subject. But then you know how men are. They're stingy when it comes to offering details."

"My family?" Elizabeth took her time sipping her tea. "There's not much to tell, really. I, um, I had a pretty typical childhood."

Interesting, Thomas got the feeling she was lying now. But after what she'd told him about tofu shish kebabs, he could see why she might want to shade the truth. Not that his grandmother would care one way or another what her parents' diet preferences were. He certainly didn't.

"You're in Ann Arbor now, I know, but where did you grow up?"

"Oh, here and there in southeast Michigan." The answer was as vague as the one she'd written on her "resume."

"It sounds like your family moved around lot," Nana Jo said. "Your father's job?"

Elizabeth sipped her tea. "More or less."

"And you have an older sister."

"A younger brother," Thomas and Elizabeth said at the same time.

"My goodness, I *am* getting old," Nana Jo said. "Somehow I managed to get that completely backward."

She sent Elizabeth a bemused smile that took a calculating turn when it reached Thomas. *Uh-oh.* He knew that look. Nana Jo sensed something was afloat.

"So, how old is your brother?" Nana Jo

picked up the plate of cookies and held it out for Elizabeth.

She selected one. "Ross is twenty-six."

"Is he married or engaged?"

"No. I... We don't see one another often."

"Oh, that's too bad. You must miss him."

"I do. Terribly."

Nana Jo made a sympathetic noise and patted the back of Elizabeth's hand. "Does he live out of state?"

"Yes. He...travels a lot. He hasn't been back to Michigan in years."

"Then your wedding will be a reunion as well. Will he be standing up?" Nana Jo asked. Nodding in Thomas's direction, she complained, "That one there won't tell me anything about the ceremony preparations. He won't even give me the date."

"Because we haven't decided yet," Thomas inserted hastily. "With our work schedules and such, it's not as easy as throwing a dart at a calendar."

"Well, surely you have some inkling of the number of groomsmen you're planning."

He glanced helplessly at Elizabeth. "I could ask Ross to be a groomsman."

"No!" She looked stricken. "I'm sorry."

"Or not."

Elizabeth apologized a second time. Her

face was flushed. Her expression miserable. "I haven't mentioned this before, Thomas, but I don't know where Ross is." Her gaze shifted to his grandmother. "My brother left—ran away from home, actually—when I was in college. He quit school and just...left."

"And you haven't heard from him since then?" Thomas asked.

"Personally, no."

"I'm sorry," Nana Jo said softly.

Thomas was more than sorry. He felt culpable in forcing the admission. He reached for her hand and knitted their fingers together before bringing it to rest against his heart. "Elizabeth, I had no idea."

She allowed the contact for a moment before pulling her hand free, ostensibly to push her breeze-blown hair back from her face. "I don't talk about it often."

"But I'm guessing you think about him and worry every day," Nana Jo said sympathetically.

"I do."

"That's the way Tommy is about his father."

He blinked in surprise. He hadn't seen the switch in subjects coming. Caught off guard. he retorted sharply, "I don't give a damn where he is or what he's doing as long as he isn't on my doorstep looking for more money so he can pay off his bar tab."

"Thomas Jonathon Waverly!"

The use of his full name pulled him up short, just as it always had when he was a child.

"I'm sorry." He expelled a breath and turned to Elizabeth and repeated his apology.

"It's forgotten," she said.

"Nothing is forgotten."

Their gazes held until a gust of wind sent paper napkins flying off the table. He and Elizabeth both rose to fetch them before they could be carried over the rail.

"I should have brought a headband," she remarked, shoving her wayward hair back from her face and settling into her seat once more.

"I'm glad you didn't." Reminding himself it was expected for him to touch her, he gave in to temptation and brushed a stray tendril off of her forehead. "I like it loose like this and a little disheveled."

"Why?" She glanced at his grandmother before laughing uncomfortably. "I mean, I look a mess."

"Hardly, my dear," Nana Jo said. "You're too pretty to look anything of the sort."

Recalling how Elizabeth had disagreed with him the one time he'd called her pretty,

Thomas half expected her to do so now. He told himself he only was forestalling her argument when he leaned over and, in a voice barely above a whisper, said, "I like it this way because it reminds me of how it looked after I had my hands in it the other night."

He was close enough to hear her breath hitch. He was smug enough to like it. He decided to press his advantage—for Nana Jo's benefit, of course—and kissed the corner of Elizabeth's mouth. Both women sighed afterward.

Nana Jo, however, had a bone to pick.

"I would remind you that it's rude not to speak loud enough so that everyone at the table can hear you, Tommy."

"Sorry." But he flashed a cocky grin that had her pursing her lips.

Still, Nana Jo accepted the apology with a nod. Then she was grinning as well. "Based on Beth's very becoming blush, I gather that whatever you whispered in her ear wasn't fit for mine anyway."

Elizabeth laughed weakly. "Still, he is being rude."

She tried to tame her hair again, even though the breeze had other plans for it. The blush staining her cheeks was, as his grandmother said, becoming. Pretty? No. At that very moment, he thought her beautiful. Inside of him, something shifted with all the subtlety of an earthquake. It was a good thing he was seated or he might have wound up losing his balance.

Especially when Nana Jo added, "Yes, but that's what happens when a man's in love. He forgets everything including his manners."

This made twice his grandmother had used the L-word. His breath caught in his throat. Hell, he could hardly drag enough of it into his lungs, until he reminded himself that he wanted his grandmother to think he was in love. The fact that she did simply meant he was playing his role superbly.

Kudos to me, he decided sourly. If his business ever folded maybe there was a career waiting for him in Hollywood.

"Are you all right?" Elizabeth asked, looking concerned as she laid a hand on his arm.

"Allergies." He coughed for effect. "Must be a lot of tree pollen in the air around here or something."

Something being the operative word.

Nana Jo frowned. "Tommy, you don't have—" She broke off abruptly then. "Goodness, Beth, where's your engagement ring?"

Thomas would have appreciated his reprieve more if his freedom from the frying pan hadn't landed him in the fire. He knew where the ring was. It was exactly where he'd left it, in the pocket of the herringbone jacket that was still in Elizabeth's possession. He cursed himself for the oversight. Meanwhile, Elizabeth looked stricken.

"I…I…" She sent him a panicked look.

"It's being sized." He reached for her left hand and caressed its knuckles with the pad of his thumb. Her fingers were so small and delicate that the lie was believable. His mother's ring never would have fit without a jeweler's adjustment.

"I see."

Nana Jo's gaze made him nervous. When he was a kid, Nana Jo always seemed to be one step ahead of him. But surely she didn't suspect…

She kept him guessing with her next question.

"I'll have to settle for a description, then. What does it look like, Beth?"

Elizabeth appeared to be the one suffering a bout of something now. The blush of a moment ago was gone along with most of her color.

"You've seen it, Nana Jo. It's Mom's ring."

He had both women's full attention now.

"You gave Beth your mother's ring? How... how lovely." But she was frowning.

Don't ask, he ordered himself. Just leave it be. But he heard himself say, "You don't seem very happy about that."

"I guess I'm just a little surprised." She sent an apologetic glance Elizabeth's way. "But in a good way, of course. In a good way. It's a lovely ring."

He recalled it now. Lovely, yes. But somehow not at all right for Elizabeth.

Still, when Nana Jo lifted her iced tea and said, "Let's have a toast, shall we?" he raised his glass as well.

"To your engagement and the start of a wonderful new life together."

Glasses clinked, smiles were exchanged. But Thomas kept thinking that as real as the moment seemed, nothing about it felt right.

CHAPTER TEN

SOMEHOW, they managed to get through the rest of the first day without further incident. For dinner, Thomas cooked burgers on the balcony's small grill to go along with the coleslaw and potato salad Nana Jo had made. They ate indoors this time. The breeze was just too strong.

After dinner, even though Nana Jo insisted they could go out if they wanted, they opted to stay in. To Thomas's dismay and Elizabeth's delight, his grandmother pulled out a stack of old photo albums.

"Don't show her the one of—"

"Too late," Nana Jo crowed. "Here's Tommy at twelve, shaving."

"Shaving at twelve."

"He didn't have a hair on his face but, bless his heart, he insisted he needed to start shaving." Nana Jo's laughter filled the condominium.

Thomas groaned louder when the page was flipped to reveal a shot of him at about fourteen dressed in a suit, a girl of the same age at his side. Hannah something. She was as tall as he was, but towered over him thanks to her hair.

"I love her 'do."

"Come on, admit it. You styled your hair the same way. All the girls did."

"Not me."

He believed her.

"First date?" Elizabeth inquired.

"School dance. She was the granddaughter of a friend of Nana Jo's."

"He holds that first fix-up against me to this day, which is why I've never again meddled in his personal affairs." When they both glanced her way, Nana Jo amended, "Much."

They finished with that album and Elizabeth pulled another from the stack.

"Not that one…" Thomas fell silent as she opened it.

A lovely brunette stared back at Elizabeth. Her hair was feathered away from her face. Her blue-green eyes were fringed with dark lashes. Elizabeth knew those eyes.

"That's Tommy's mom, my Lynn." Nana Jo's expression wasn't sad so much as resigned. "That picture was taken not long before the accident. She was a beautiful young woman. When she walked in a room, she lit it up with her smile."

"I can see that." Elizabeth chanced a glance in Thomas's direction. She expected to find him frowning, but the corners of his mouth were starting to curve.

He tapped the photograph. "Right before this picture was taken she'd grounded me from television for a week."

"For what?" Nana Jo wanted to know.

"I broke a glass baking dish."

"That doesn't sound like Lynn."

His smile bloomed in full. "I was using it to start a worm farm and dropped it on the kitchen floor. Worms were everywhere when Mom came in, and company was due in less than an hour."

Elizabeth laughed. His grandmother joined in. Thomas shook his head on a smile. "She was something. The day my grounding officially ended, she got out an old shoebox, lined it with plastic and then the pair of us went out to the flower garden and hunted up more worms."

"Lynn did that?"

"She wore a pair of gloves, but, yeah. The only time I recall her freaking out was when a big daddy longlegs climbed up her arm."

"My girl hated spiders," Nana Jo said. "Can't say that I blame her. I loathe the things myself."

Lynn Waverly might have hated spiders, but she'd loved her child more. Elizabeth could picture them, mother and son, on their knees in the dirt, small spades in hand, turning over the earth and squealing in delight—whether real or manufactured—over their finds.

"She sounds like the kind of mother I hope to be someday. Very hands-on. Very involved." Not the passive parents her own had been.

"Then you will be, my dear," Nana Jo said with such certainty that Elizabeth had no option but to believe, even if in the past she'd worried that Delphine's hands-off style might be hard-wired into her genes.

They continued with the photo albums after that, working their way through the entire stack.

"I hope we're not boring you," Thomas said at one point.

"Hardly." And she meant it. She liked hearing the stories that went along with the pictures. She liked hearing his laughter mingled with his grandmother's as they reminisced over the past.

A little later, when he excused himself to

use the bathroom, Nana Jo pulled Elizabeth aside.

"I want to thank you, Beth."

"For what?"

"For Tommy's laughter and easy smile. We haven't looked through those albums in years. Especially that particular album. He's avoided talking about Lynn. In fact, he's avoided all of the memories that came before the accident, whether good or bad. Any time I've brought up his mother, he's changed the subject or found a reason to cut the conversation short."

"I didn't realize."

"After the accident, when I went to live with Tommy and his father, I was appalled that Hoyt had gotten rid of every last picture of her. But later, when Hoyt was gone and it was just Tommy and me, I started noticing that the pictures that I'd put out disappeared, especially the ones of the three of them looking so happy. I took my cue from him and tucked most of them away. And I stopped talking about Lynn, especially with him. It seemed to make him so sad."

Elizabeth wondered if in addition to making Thomas sad, he was worried that it made his grandmother sad. It was his way of trying to protect her, even if it had done the opposite.

"I'm sorry." Elizabeth squeezed Nana Jo's hand.

"I've been, too. Sorry for both of us. I miss my daughter. All these years later, the ache doesn't go away. But tonight…" The older woman's eyes misted and she squeezed Elizabeth's hand in return. "It was like Lynn was here with us."

"She was. In both of you."

"You're good for him, Beth. So very good for him. I can see why he loves you."

Elizabeth's smile faltered. She wished she could agree.

Elizabeth woke early and stretched on the bed. She'd slept well, incredibly well, all things considered. She credited the fresh air and the little sachet of lavender that Nana Jo had tucked under the pillow. The woman thought of everything.

Dressed in a pair of navy blue shorts and a sleeveless white blouse, Elizabeth left the bedroom. Then she gathered up her toiletries, hoping to scoot into the bathroom before she was seen. The scent of freshly brewed coffee hit her as soon as she opened the bedroom door.

Someone else was an early riser. A glance at the couch confirmed that it wasn't Thomas.

He was still asleep, both feet sticking over the armrest, arms above his head. The blanket Nana Jo had provided him with was still neatly folded on the coffee table. It had been too warm for that, even with the breeze. As for the sheet, he'd kicked it off and it lay in a heap on the floor. He wore pajamas…of a sort: a white T-shirt and a pair of lightweight athletic shorts. The shirt's hem was pulled up just enough that she caught a glimpse of toned abs.

She was openly ogling them when Nana Jo slipped up behind her and said, "He gets that lean build from the O'Keefe side. My husband was the same way."

Elizabeth started. The older woman moved like a cat. "I…I…was just going to wash my face."

Nana Jo chuckled. Elizabeth thought she heard the older woman say, "Use cold water."

Since it was Elizabeth's first visit to Charlevoix, Nana Jo and Thomas insisted on showing her around town that afternoon. Walking along sidewalks crowded with tourists kept conversation to a minimum, a fact for which Elizabeth was grateful. Given the roiling mix of emotions she was experiencing, she was happy to window-shop and ooh and aah over the sights.

She might even have enjoyed herself if not for the loose hold Thomas kept on her hand as they strolled along. The only time he let go was when they entered a store, and then only so he could open the door, after which his hand would find the small of her back, guiding her along inside. It was such simple contact, but it kept stirring up needs, not all of them physical, though those were the most obvious. With her hormones threatening to go from simmer to boil, the stark line she'd drawn between reality and make-believe was turning into a blurry mess.

She'd promised him that she wouldn't pull away from his touch, and she'd been keeping her word. She'd also promised herself that she wouldn't get *carried* away. Well, so much for that vow. She was. Even though she was doing her darnedest to keep her feet planted firmly on the ground, her imagination kept taking flight, threatening to pull her heart right along with it.

But who could blame her?

She'd found Thomas tempting even before he'd transformed himself into the besotted bridegroom-to-be for his grandmother's benefit. Now, with his charm kicked into hyperdrive, it was ever so easy to believe that his one major flaw was fixable.

Except that it wasn't.

He didn't want a long-term relationship with the possibility of a lifetime commitment, no matter what his pretty words and solicitous behavior indicated now. While she hadn't been actively seeking love when she walked into his office that day, she knew what she wanted for her future, and it was the whole shebang—a husband and a couple of kids to go with the dog she already had. She wanted permanence, continuity, the kind of peace of mind her vagabond childhood had lacked despite her parents' unwavering devotion to one another.

Thomas couldn't provide that. He might like Elizabeth. He might even be interested in her romantically beyond their arrangement, since he seemed genuinely attracted to her, a fact that, in and of itself, caused her pulse to quicken and need to pool. But whatever happened between them wouldn't last. It would come with an expiration date that he had predetermined.

He ended things before they became "messy." He'd told her that, had made it abundantly clear. She would be a fool to allow anything to transpire between them. Yet, strolling hand-in-hand down a sidewalk on a warm sunny day, she found herself wishing for the impossible, because take away that one flaw of his—major as it was—and the man was perfect and, when she was around him, he made Elizabeth feel that way, too.

"Here's the restaurant I was thinking we could eat dinner at this evening," Nana Jo said, stopping outside a pair of bright red doors. A framed menu hung to one side. Pointing at it, she said, "Why don't you both take a look and tell me what you think."

"I think I'm shocked that you're not going to cook for us yourself," Thomas teased. "After making the burgers on the grill last night, I've been looking forward to a home-cooked meal. It's been ages since I last had one."

Nana Jo frowned before turning to Elizabeth with a quizzical expression. "Don't you cook, Beth?"

Uh-oh. She felt Thomas squeeze her hand. In desperation or in reassurance?

"Actually, I do," she replied truthfully. Feeling a little bit rebellious, she added, "Quite well, in fact."

"Oh?"

"I took a six-week course on Italian cuisine offered through the public school district's community education program a few years ago. I was tired of eating stuff that came out of a box or from the freezer."

"Smart cookie." Nana Jo tapped an arthritic finger to one of her temples.

"Yes. But our work schedules," Thomas began, going for the save, "sometimes they conflict. Other times, well, Elizabeth is just too tired to whip up a big meal after a long day at the office."

"Office? I thought you told me that Beth worked at a bank, Tommy? And, I've got to ask, why are you calling her Elizabeth? I noticed that yesterday, too."

Oh, he had both feet in it now. Still, Elizabeth had no intention of lying to bail him out. She told his grandmother, "Perhaps he confused me with one of the many other women he dated in the past. There were dozens of them from what I understand."

Nana Jo chuckled at that. Thomas didn't, but then the joke was at his expense. Even so, he did appear grateful no longer to be in the hot seat.

"I can promise you both I haven't confused Elizabeth with anyone else." His gaze turned intense. "That would be impossible."

His pronouncement caused her heart to squeeze and that was before he went on. "As for why I call her by her full name of Elizabeth, well, that's how I've come to see her. Elizabeth is a strong name. It fits a woman of such indomitable will and determination perfectly. I won't make the mistake of judging a book by its cover ever again."

"Thomas." Whether or not the words were scripted for his grandmother's benefit, Elizabeth was touched by them.

He continued, "Right after graduating from Michigan State University with a teaching degree, she founded a nonprofit agency whose goal is to foster literacy in adults. It's been going strong for a decade and will for many years to come thanks to her efforts to raise funds for an endowment. As you can see, Nana Jo, my Elizabeth is quite remarkable."

It wasn't his possessive reference that caused emotions to clog her throat, though it certainly was having an effect on her heart rate. No, it was the admiration evident in his expression. He meant it. Every word.

"Thomas," she said again.

This time, he leaned over and kissed her soundly on the mouth.

When he pulled back, Nana Jo was beaming.

"What an accomplishment!" she exclaimed, pulling Elizabeth in for a hug. "And you're so young!" She slapped at Thomas's arm. "I can't believe you didn't tell me, especially when it's obvious that you're so proud of her."

"I am proud of her."

"And rightfully so." Nana Jo made a *tutting* sound. "Madeline Stevens thinks her grandson is marrying well simply because his fiancée's family can trace its roots back to the *Mayflower*. What kind of an accomplishment is that? A mere accident of birth is what that is. I can't wait till our next bridge night so I can exercise my bragging rights."

Elizabeth remained flattered and flummoxed and that was before Thomas kissed her a second time and said, "I'm a lucky man."

"And a smart man if you keep telling yourself that," his grandmother advised. Turning back to the restaurant, she said, "So, about dinner, does this place look good to you? I've had their herb-crusted trout and blackened whitefish before. Both were excellent. And I've heard positive things about their steaks, though I steer clear of red meat these days for obvious reasons."

Elizabeth turned her gaze to the menu, grateful to have something to occupy her mind rather than the way she'd felt pulled to Thomas's side. Three words caught her attention immediately: formal attire required.

"The cuisine sounds delicious, but I'm afraid all of the outfits I brought to wear are way too casual," she told Nana Jo.

"I didn't pack a jacket, either," Thomas said.

His grandmother wasn't dissuaded. "Your navy sports coat is still hanging in the bedroom closet, I believe. As for you, Elizabeth, even a simple dress will do. No need for ball gowns or the like. The owners just put that there to keep tourists from stopping in wearing swimsuits on their way back from a day at the beach."

"I didn't pack any dresses."

Thomas chuckled. His arm was still around her. "You saw her bag, Nana. My Elizabeth packs light."

She was still digesting his "My Elizabeth" comment when his grandmother said, "Let's go shopping, then. My treat. Consider it a gift to celebrate your engagement."

"Oh, that's not necessary." She should have known arguing was pointless.

"I'm an old woman and it would give me great pleasure. Besides, I insist."

And as Nana Jo had already made clear, once she made up her mind there was little else one could do but shut up and agree.

"There's a store just up the way that carries some lovely dresses. And shoes, too. Back before arthritis got the best of me, I loved to wear high heels. I must have had at least two dozen pairs. I would have had more, but my closet wouldn't hold any more. That was before I moved here with a big walk-in one that's larger than the kitchen was in my first house."

"Do I have to come along?" Thomas wanted to know. "Shopping is really more of a female thing."

"You may be excused if it's all right with Beth, *er*, Elizabeth."

She made a flicking gesture with her fingers. "By all means, go and do something manly."

Nana Jo rubbed her hands together and her eyes lit with excitement. "Oh, this is going to be so much fun."

Elizabeth had never been much of a shopper, although every so often when Mel went to the mall in Ann Arbor, she insisted on dragging her along. Even then, she found the vast array of color choices and styles overwhelming, which made staying in her safe set of hues all the more appealing.

But the store Nana Jo had in mind was small, its merchandise neatly arranged with coordinating accessories within handy reach, and its staff helpful and eager to please. They were met at the door with beaming smiles and promptly assigned a saleswoman, who clearly knew Thomas's grandmother well.

"Mrs. O'Keefe, how nice to see you today," the young woman named Kendra enthused. "We got in some new Pima cotton sweater sets last week. I put one in your size in red in the back. I know how you favor that color."

"Thanks, dear. That's lovely. I'll have a look at it in a minute. Right now I'm here with my grandson's fiancée to see about a dress for dinner tonight. We're going to Edward's."

"Thomas is getting married?" The question came not from the salesclerk but from an attractive woman with flowing blond hair who stood just to their right. She'd had her back to them when they arrived, working her way through a rack of sundresses.

"Oh, Cecelia. I didn't see you there. Hello."

"Mrs. O'Keefe."

They shook hands. No bone-crushing hug from Nana Jo for this one, Elizabeth thought smugly. But then since the lush-figured woman stood half a head taller than Nana Jo, the hug wouldn't have had the same effect anyway.

"This is Elizabeth Morris."

One corner of the woman's red-slicked

mouth turned up. In a wry voice, she replied, "Better known as the woman who managed to get Thomas Waverly to forsake bachelorhood. I stand in awe."

Cecelia didn't look awed. She looked put out and slightly amused.

"It's nice to meet you," Elizabeth said, even though the jury was still out on that one.

"I didn't realize Thomas had been ill."

"Why, he's fine," Nana Jo replied on a frown.

"Healthy as a…stallion," Elizabeth added, raising both women's eyebrows and her own color. Stallion, horse—they were the same thing.

"I'm glad to hear it." Cecelia's tone suggested otherwise. "I just assumed he must have suffered a near-death experience to change his mind on the subject. He was quite adamant about it when we dated last summer."

And then she was dumped, no doubt. Elizabeth wanted to feel sorry for the woman, but sympathy was a difficult emotion to muster under Cecelia's condescending stare. Her expression made it clear she wasn't as hurt that Thomas was settling down as she was annoyed that he was settling down with someone like Elizabeth.

"I suspect his change of heart had to do

with finding the right woman," Nana Jo re-marked. Her innocent expression made the barb appear unintended, but Elizabeth wondered if that really were the case. She'd already figured out that Josephine O'Keefe was a clever woman. After all, she had her very bright grandson believing she was heading toward eternity.

Cecelia left abruptly after that.

"She's a viper, that one," Nana Jo said. "Her parents bought a condo in the next building over two summers ago. She had her cap set for Thomas the moment she saw his fancy car pull up. Status is everything to her. Her parents are the same way. It's got to be designer labels and the latest trends or they're not having any of it." Nana Jo's lips pursed. "I was quite disappointed when I heard Thomas was dating her. Heard, mind you. He never brought her to see me on his own initiative, although every time his car showed up in the parking lot she soon found her way to my door."

"She's very pretty." The comment slipped out.

"Yes. Some of the most poisonous creatures on the planet are." To Kendra, Nana Jo said, "I hope I didn't cost you a sale."

"Not likely." The young woman rolled her

eyes. "Cecelia comes in regularly and tries on half of the store, only to leave after complaining about our pitiful lack of inventory." She lowered her voice and admitted, "The other salesgirls and I draw straws to see who will have to wait on her. She's a lot of work and very little commission."

"Then I'd say you're well rid of her, too. Now about Elizabeth's outfit for tonight…"

Thomas hadn't wanted to go shopping with the women, but after circling around the block twice and pretending to be absorbed in a storefront display of hand-tied fishing flies, he gave in to curiosity and headed to the store where Nana Jo had taken Elizabeth.

He had two concerns. First, that Nana Jo, who preferred nautical themes and colors, would talk Elizabeth into a sailoresque outfit.

And second, that Elizabeth would think she needed to go for something flashy. He recalled how she'd looked on their first "date," if the outing could be called such a thing. The short dress with its horizontal flounces was more along the lines of attire the women of his acquaintance wore, and it definitely had caught his attention. She'd looked downright amazing in it. But there was something to be said for her conservative outfits. His mouth curved thinking of them. Prim as they were, they left his imagination to wonder what she had on underneath. Pink lace came to mind again as it had with disturbing regularity since that evening in her living room.

With that image taunting his libido, he stopped for ice cream on his way to the store. Instead of ordering his usual chocolate in a cone, he ordered plain vanilla, which he had the girl behind the counter sprinkle with chocolate chips.

He still had half the cone to go when he reached the shop, so he waited outside while he finished it. It wasn't brain freeze he experienced but something more primal when, through the window, he saw her step out of one of the dressing rooms. The tailored cotton shirt dress hit right above her knees, and was cinched in at the waist with a wide fabric belt. It was the epitome of conservative when it came to the cut, but not the color: red.

Not the nautical red that his grandmother liked. This red was more like chili peppers and packed as much punch. He was reminded of the heat in that Szechwan dish they'd shared in her kitchen. His mouth had burned then. Something else was on fire now.

He felt like a voyeur. He should just go in and quit acting like a Peeping Tom, er,

Thomas. But he remained on the sidewalk while tourists strolled past and his ice cream melted, and watched through the glass as the salesgirl presented Elizabeth with a pair of tan shoes. The heels weren't stiletto height, but he'd judge them to be nearly three inches, and despite the neutral color they were sexy thanks to an open toe. He was too far away to see if her nails were polished when she slipped out of her canvas flats and slid the heels on. For some reason he knew they would be. A woman who wore lacy pink undergarments would take the time to paint her toes. Why that thought should excite him so much, Thomas wasn't sure. He only knew that it did. And then some.

Elizabeth took a few steps and he lost sight of her behind a circular rack of bathing suits. Then she was back, grinning madly, and looking more relaxed than he'd seen her look since their arrival the day before. His grandmother was grinning, too. He told himself it was worth it, the lies and the subterfuge, to see Nana Jo looking this carefree and fit. Eventually, she would be disappointed when the wedding she'd chattered about for months never happened. He ignored the stab of guilt. And it *was* guilt. What else could it be? Certainly not his own disappointment.

Nana Jo glanced over then and must have spied him. She pointed his way, said something, and then Elizabeth's gaze turned in his direction as well. Her smile didn't quite disappear, but her expression grew serious.

Busted, Thomas thought. He waved nonchalantly, hoping to cover his embarrassment, but wound up feeling like an even bigger fool when what was left of his melted ice cream slid off the cone and plopped on the top of his shoe.

For the remainder of the afternoon, Thomas felt self-conscious and it had nothing to do with the sticky smudge that remained on the top of his sneaker. He felt oddly vulnerable.

He knew why Elizabeth had agreed to pose as his fiancée. She needed the hefty donation he'd promised for her charity's endowment fund. But a question was now nagging at him. Would she be interested in him for real if the carrot of a hefty donation for her charity were no longer dangling in front of her nose?

She seemed to like him, and, given the way she'd responded to his kisses, the sexual attraction he felt wasn't all one-sided. But…

In a very short period of time, they'd gotten to know one another better than Thomas could recall getting to know any of the other women with whom he'd spent a couple months. He credited the fact that Elizabeth was easy to talk to. They had shared some laughs and traded enough basic information to play the role of an engaged couple for a weekend. Still, he knew he'd barely scratched the surface. He wanted to know more. Much more. Beyond Chinese takeout preferences and toenail polish and undergarment choices.

No wonder he was feeling self-conscious and vulnerable. He'd always preferred women to start out as mysteries and remain that way. All of the little discoveries that couples made about one another during a relationship resulted in intimacy. Thomas strove to keep things casual with no deep emotional ties to untangle when it came time to break things off.

But Elizabeth intrigued him. God help him, but ties, emotional and otherwise, were starting to seem mighty tempting where she was concerned.

CHAPTER ELEVEN

Nana Jo had made reservations at the restaurant for seven o'clock that evening, which gave them all plenty of time to relax and get ready when they returned to the condo.

His grandmother decided to lie down for a short nap. Thomas and Elizabeth decided to shower before getting dressed. Since they were sharing the guest bathroom, he told her to go first.

That was a mistake.

She didn't take long. In fact, she was in and out in record time.

"All yours," she said when they passed in the hallway afterward.

Her hair was wrapped turban style in a towel and she was wrapped in a short terry-cloth robe that offered a tantalizing view of her legs and not nearly enough of the rest of her. His imagination got busy filling in the blanks, doing the job a little too well while he shaved. He nicked his chin twice with the razor.

He decided to make the shower a long, cold one, but even the chilly spray couldn't keep his imagination in check. It was a little too easy to picture her under the same pulsating water, her skin slick and inviting, slim limbs wrapped around him much the same way her scent was.

Thomas inhaled deeply and groaned. He'd caught faint whiffs of her fragrance during the day when he'd pulled her close or leaned in to tell her something. Now, it surrounded him in the shower stall. Whatever brand of shampoo or body wash she used, it was tying him into knots.

Those knots tightened after he finished up his lengthy shower and stepped out. On the counter next to the sink he spotted the travel-sized bottle of shampoo standing next to a small makeup case.

At home, with other women, he always made a point to discourage such items from showing up in his bathroom. They implied too much permanence for his comfort. Technically, this wasn't his bathroom. Perhaps that explained why he found himself more curious than wary. He took the cap off the bottle and sniffed. This was it. The scent was fresh and straightforward…just like the woman.

When the knock sounded he nearly dropped the bottle.

"Yes?"

"It's Elizabeth. I'm sorry to bother you, but I was wondering if you could hand me the makeup case I left in there?" she asked through the closed door. "I want to freshen up the polish on my toenails."

Of course she did. He swallowed and glanced toward the bag as if it contained the average man's equivalent of kryptonite.

Elizabeth nibbled the inside of her cheek while she waited for Thomas to respond. Instead of replying, however, he opened the bathroom door. And not just to pass her the case. Interestingly, no steam escaped from the bathroom despite his shower, which had gone on for quite some time—hence her decision to knock. Her nails would need time to dry before she slipped her feet into the new shoes. But the lack of steam wasn't what had her full attention. The man did.

Instead of a robe, he wore a towel wrapped around his hips, hooked low on his waist, below his belly button. The towel may have been pink, but his masculinity was never in

question. To think she'd found so tantalizing that mere glimpse of his abs she'd gotten
while he'd slept on the couch.

Oh, my!

She should maintain eye contact, Elizabeth
thought. For that matter, she should grab the
bag from his hand and return to the guest
room posthaste. But she stood opposite him
and gaped openly, though at least she had the
presence of mind to close her mouth. The man
was perfection, with sculpted arms and the
kind of chest and abdomen that deserved to
be showcased in a fitness program's "after"
photographs.

"See something you like?" There was a hint
of challenge in his tone along with amusement.

Elizabeth saw no point in lying, but that
didn't mean she intended to stroke his ego.
"Let's just say that I see why you have no
problem attracting women."

"I've always assumed it was my good manners."

"That, too. Women find a man's…good
manners very hard to resist."

His lips twitched. "Does that include you?"

"Are you angling for a compliment?"

She tilted her head to one side. Her hair,
which was still damp, fell across her forehead.

She held her breath when he reached over and pushed it aside. Would she ever get used to his touch? Did she want to?

"An answer will do."

She was playing with fire, but instead of trying to douse it, she opted to feed it. "I don't think it's any great secret that I find you attractive, Thomas."

"Or that it's mutual," he added on a smile.

"Yes. I picked up on that as well. We have some definite chemistry," she allowed.

"Chemistry." His chuckle was dry and seemed self-directed. He rested one forearm against the doorjamb and leaned on it. "I like you, Elizabeth."

It was hardly an earth-shattering announcement, but it caused her insides to quake. Just what was he saying? The words were clear, but not their meaning, given his history. Given *their* history, brief as it was. Or maybe their conversation was nothing more than friendly banter made to seem more intimate by the fact they were both half-naked.

"I've been told I'm likeable. I took a Dale Carnegie course just out of college to improve interpersonal relationships and strengthen my communication skills."

"I also like your sense of humor," he added. "It's dry."

"You mentioned that before."

"Some things are worth repeating."

He levered away from the jamb and set the makeup case aside. She'd seen that look in his eyes before. She knew what it meant. He was going to kiss her. Without his grandmother present it wasn't going to be PG, either. And she was going to let him.

Except that he bypassed her lips and lowered his mouth to the side of her neck, working his way lower. Teeth scraped lightly across the spot where her pulse was hammering so crazily that she wondered if he could hear it. Then he was moving lower, stopping only when he reached the point where the robe's lapels crossed between her breasts.

"I'm dying to know what you have on beneath this," he murmured against her skin. His breath licked at her flesh like flames.

"I have a feeling we would both regret it if you managed to find out," she whispered, amazed that she hadn't melted into a puddle of hormones much the way his ice cream had melted earlier in the day. She'd been amused then. She was dead serious now.

Thomas issued a mild expletive that apparently served as agreement. He straightened enough that his face was inches from hers. No apologies followed his oath this time. Elizabeth considered that an odd sort of victory.

"Maybe you could just tell me then."

"Will that be enough for you?"

"What do you think?"

She knew the answer. She also knew that eventually, if things were allowed to progress between them, he would get his fill, even as she would crave more—physically and emotionally. She forced herself to remember that.

"We'd better get dressed. Your grandmother will be ready soon. She could walk out of her bedroom at any moment." Elizabeth glanced down the hall at Nana Jo's closed door after saying so.

"You're right," Thomas agreed reluctantly. Even so, he took his time readjusting her lapels, before dropping a kiss on her cheek.

Dinner was lovely. The food was superb, the service impeccable and the company…? Elizabeth had absolutely no complaints to register there. Thomas was his usual charming and solicitous self, though she caught a considering glance or two. His grandmother's presence ensured the conversation remained topical rather than intimate.

It was far from boring, though. Indeed, Elizabeth liked seeing this side of Thomas.

He was so unguarded and open. And, just her luck, all the more appealing.

"You're making moon eyes at my grandson again," Nana Jo remarked on a pleased smile.

"I…I…"

"It's all right, dear. He's been making them right back when you're not watching."

The woman was sharp as a tack. And wily, Elizabeth realized after a couple of her friends stopped by their table to say hello.

"Jean, would you and Barbara mind giving me a ride home? That way these young people can stay and have dessert. It's been a long day with a lot of walking." Where she'd been bright-eyed and laughing a moment earlier, Nana Jo now yawned. "I tire out so easily these days."

Elizabeth couldn't be sure, but she thought she saw one of Nana Jo's friends elbow the other one in the ribs.

"I'll get the check," Thomas said, already raising his hand to signal the waiter.

His grandmother reached for it and gave it a squeeze. "That's sweet, my boy, but I won't hear of it. You both stay, have dessert. The red velvet cake the couple over there is sharing looks delicious." The couple in question wasn't just sharing a dessert; they were sharing a fork and very nearly a chair. From the looks of things, later on they would be sharing a whole heck of a lot more. Nana Jo winked. "Makes me wish I were younger and not just because of my restricted diet."

"We'll get a couple slices to go," Thomas said. "You can have a couple bites of mine. Your doctor doesn't need to know."

"That's generous, but no. The two of you stay," Nana Jo insisted again, this time rising to her feet. "And don't feel like you need to rush home. I'll probably just take my heart pill and go straight to bed. Take a walk on the beach after you finish up here. Take advantage of the moonlight."

"I think we've been had," Elizabeth said once they were alone.

"Maybe." But he glanced anxiously toward the door through which his grandmother had just exited. "Still, it's hard not to worry about her. She is eighty-one."

And in better shape than some women who were half her age. But Elizabeth only nodded. He had a blind spot a mile wide where his grandmother's health was concerned. It was endearing.

The waiter came, and they ordered dessert and coffee. Elizabeth chose a tartlet topped with an assortment of fresh, locally grown berries.

"That almost qualifies as health food," Thomas teased. "Not to mention one of the recommended daily servings of fresh fruit."

"It's all I saved room for."

"That's too bad." To the waiter, he said, "I'll have the red velvet cake. The thickest slice you've got."

Once they were alone again, his teasing expression sobered. "I like that dress, by the way. And the shoes."

So he'd said. Twice now. And he'd made an interesting remark about her painted toes. Between that and his earlier stated curiosity regarding her undergarments, it was a wonder Elizabeth had gotten through dinner without choking on her grilled sea bass.

"Thank you. Mel's been after me to buy some new clothes." She plucked at the tips of the lapels. "I think she would approve. Well, at least of the color. The style is probably a little boring."

"No offense to your friend, but I'm glad your tastes aren't the same as hers. And that dress isn't boring. It, and you, have my full attention."

Even as she reveled in the words, she wished he wouldn't say things like that. They made that line between fantasy and reality keep going fuzzy. The waiter returned with their coffee and assured them their desserts would be along shortly.

"It was very kind of your grandmother to buy everything. If she had her way, I would have a new purse, too." She shook her head in wonder at the force that was Josephine O'Keefe. "I still think I should repay her."

He poured some cream into his cup and stirred as he shook his head. "She won't let you."

"I was thinking I'd just leave a check for the total in the guest bedroom for her to find after we leave in the morning."

The corners of his mouth turned down in consideration. "Nah. She'll rip it up and be insulted. They're a gift, Elizabeth. It made her happy to give them to you. Accept them graciously."

She sighed. Arguing with either of them would be pointless. And rude. "I'll send her a bouquet of flowers as a thank-you, then."

"She'll like that. Make them stargazer lilies. They're her favorite." He took a sip of his coffee.

Elizabeth added creamer to her own cup. "I don't like deceiving her, Thomas. I said that from the outset, but I like it even less now that I know her."

"Then you understand how I feel, but—"

"But you're going to continue lying to her."

He frowned. It was guilt and concern she saw in his expression, much more than irritation. "You know my reasons."

"I do." And she knew he believed them. Just as he believed his reasons for steering clear of commitment. He was wrong on both counts, but that was something he had to discover for himself. Still… "I really think you should tell her the truth."

"What is the truth, Elizabeth?" He sounded genuinely confused.

She blinked in surprise and ticked off the obvious. "We're not engaged. We're not even dating. We barely know one another."

His expression turned oddly stubborn. Instead of denying her statements, he said, "I think I know you pretty well, better than I've allowed myself to get to know most women."

She sat back in her chair, wary of both the delight curling through her belly and the interest brewing in his eyes. "We met on Monday," she reminded him…reminded them both.

He was undeterred. "Let me give it a shot."

She lifted her hands palm-side up. "Well, then, by all means."

Before he could start, their desserts arrived. The tart, with its topping of fresh blueberries, blackberries and raspberries, looked delicious.

But it was the lush confection the waiter set in front of Thomas that had her mouth watering. It was pure indulgence on a gold-rimmed china plate and every bit as tempting as the man who was now studying her.

"Where were we?" It sounded very much like a challenge.

"You were going to dazzle me with your knowledge of my person."

He picked up his fork and pointed the tines in her direction. "There's that dry sense of humor again, tinged with just enough sarcasm that you're probably already feeling guilty about it and wanting to apologize."

She popped a fat raspberry in her mouth and rolled her eyes.

"I'm not feeling guilty." *Much.*

His smile was smug. "You are and I like that about you. You're careful with other people's feelings. You're also regretting your dessert choice."

"I am not." To prove it, she cut into the tartlet with the side of her fork and then scooped both it and a juicy blueberry into her mouth. *"Mmm."*

His brows rose. Interest smoldered in his eyes. Regrets? Elizabeth still didn't have a single one.

"Maybe *regret* isn't the right word," he

said. "You went with the berries not only because they're delicious, but because they're good for you. No trans-fats or whatever the media have determined the big health threat to be at the moment. You'll probably leave half of that tartlet on your plate." Okay, that had been her plan. "But you wish you'd ordered the red velvet cake."

"Then why didn't I?" she asked, a little unnerved by his accurate assessment. Not to mention unnerved by the close attention he paid even when he didn't seem to be.

"The reason you didn't is because you're the sort of woman who plays it safe."

He had her on the cake, but she disagreed with the rest. "How can you say that? I'm here with you, pretending to be your fiancée, aren't I? I wouldn't exactly call that playing it safe."

"My grandmother's gone, Elizabeth. It's just the two of us sitting here now. Well, and a room full of strangers. There's no need to pretend anything." His eyes narrowed seductively. "Or maybe that's the risk you mean since you spent the last couple days leading up to this trip avoiding me."

"We talked."

"Email, voice mail and one brief conversation during which you turned me down for a date." When she opened her mouth to reply, he held up a hand to stop her. "And last night you retreated to the guest room as soon as my grandmother called it a night."

Direct hits all. So she shot back and said, "You don't strike me as the sort of man who takes a lot of chances, either."

She was thinking of his relationships, though she stopped short of saying so out loud. The muscle that ticked in his jaw told her he got the reference anyway.

"Maybe. But we're not talking about me. You can grill me another time."

"Don't think I won't hold you to that."

"I know you will. I would never make the mistake of underestimating you, Elizabeth. You're the one who does that. I wish you wouldn't. God knows, you shouldn't. I meant it earlier when I told my grandmother how much I admire your determination and success."

Oh, yes, he paid way too close attention. Feeling vulnerable, she asked, "Are you done with your evaluation of me?"

He wasn't put off by her prickly tone. "Just starting. You're far too fascinating to sum up that quickly. With you, I find I want to take my time."

He took another bite of his cake. Despite her best efforts, Elizabeth licked her lips. His smile was smug, but so darn sexy that she found it impossible to be irritated, especially when he cut off another bite and fed it to her. For a man who supposedly didn't do intimate, he was doing a damned fine imitation.

"I thought time was the enemy when it came to women. We wouldn't want things to get messy."

He frowned. But all he said was, "Do you want another bite?"

"A small one."

While she savored it, he continued, "You were and remain the sort of person who colors inside the lines. Taking risks doesn't come naturally to you, but you're willing to stick out your neck if the reasons suit you. You like to help people. You want to save them."

"You don't need a crystal ball to figure that out given the line of work I'm in, not to mention our current set of circumstances."

"Maybe." He went on. "You like to blend in."

She laughed as a cover for her discomfort over the accuracy of his comment and pointed out, "I'm wearing red right now. It's hard to blend in wearing red."

"Yes, but if you really wanted to stand out in that color, you would have chosen a dress that fit snugly or ended midthigh or was cut low enough to offer a peek of cleavage."

"I don't want to attract that kind of attention. Besides, I don't have the kind of figure that lends itself to the sort of dress you're talking about."

"I don't know about that." Thomas's memory reeled back a couple of hours. "You did a pretty good job with that bathrobe earlier."

Her face turned as scarlet as the cake. "The women you date probably all look like they just stepped away from a fashion photo shoot."

"But we're not talking about me or them," he reminded her again.

"Well, I'm not in their league."

He didn't want her to be, and it had nothing to do with convincing his grandmother they were a couple.

"See, that's where you've got it backward, Elizabeth. They're not in *your* league." He wasn't trying to boost her self-esteem. It was true. "In addition to underestimating yourself, you're hard on yourself."

She didn't wait for him to offer her cake this time. She reached over with her own fork and stole some. What was it about that simple act that turned him on?

"So, I'm a perfectionist. It's not exactly a character flaw, although some people might see it that way."

Thomas shook his head. "It's not the same thing. I thought it might be at first. You have such drive, such focus. People like that tend to be compulsive in certain respects. But there's more to it in your case than seeking perfection."

She shifted uncomfortably in her seat. "I don't know what you mean."

"When we first met I asked you what made you decide to start Literacy Liaisons. Do you remember your answer?"

She laughed, though he detected nerves. "Of course I do. As I said, that was only a matter of days ago."

He didn't laugh. "You told me you saw a need."

"That's right."

"Care to tell me what exactly that need was?" He had a good idea now.

"That should be obvious, Thomas." He merely raised his brows and waited. "All around us, in a country that spends billions of dollars to provide free and mandated education to the public, there are people who cannot read. It impacts their lives, their relationships and their earning potential. It holds them back."

"Ross can't read."

"Wh-what?"

She'd spoken so little about her family to Thomas that it was clear she was unprepared for Thomas to draw lines between the random dots she'd provided and come up with a clear picture.

"Your brother. He can't read, can he?"

She set down her fork, dabbed her mouth with the linen napkin that had been spread over her lap. It was a moment before she spoke. "He can read. At a third-grade level, and that's probably being generous."

"That's why he left school and then left home."

"No, Thomas." She shook her head, her expression filled with sadness and something more damning when she told him, "He left home because of me."

"Elizabeth—"

"No. It's true. I was in college, studying to be a teacher of all things, when I found out that Ross was functionally illiterate and had dropped out of school. I was livid. I went home the first weekend I could and started in on him. 'You need to do this. You need to do that.' I drove him away with all of my pushing and nagging."

"You did it out of love."

"That doesn't matter. It backfired, badly."

This conversation was backfiring badly, Thomas realized. He'd intended to show her…hell, he wasn't sure what he'd intended to show her. Or why it mattered so much. All he knew was that *she* mattered.

"He phones our parents from time to time or has someone else drop them a note, but he's never contacted me."

Thomas chose his words carefully. "He's probably just embarrassed."

"That's what Mel says."

"What do your parents say?"

"My parents." She shifted back in her seat on a sigh. "They see nothing wrong with the situation. They never saw anything wrong with the situation, even when he was young enough that they could have done something about it."

"Are you sure they didn't try?"

"Not hard enough." Her laughter was brittle. "I love them, but their child-rearing methods, to say nothing of their lifestyle, leave a lot to be desired. Their motto was and remains live and let live. The fact that Ross doesn't have a permanent address and can't hold down a regular job doesn't bother them in the least. They actually thought it was exciting when he called from Utah a few years ago to say that he'd joined up with one of those carnivals that travel from town to town."

"Is that where he is now? Utah?"

"Honestly, I don't know." She shook her head sadly. "My parents barely pass along any information and I've stopped asking. I keep hoping…" Her laughter turned harsh. "I keep hoping he'll write to me."

"It's not your fault that he can't read. Or that he left home and has chosen the lifestyle he has."

"I went about it all wrong," she insisted. "I pushed him away."

"You can't push someone away by caring too much, Elizabeth."

Her gaze locked with his. "Yes, you can, Thomas. You're proof of that. It's the reason you've used to end all of your relationships. And, if I were to let myself fall for you, it would be the reason you'd use to end ours."

CHAPTER TWELVE

IT WAS nearly ten when they left the restaurant. Thomas decided the wisest course of action would be to head straight back to his grandmother's condo. Despite Nana Jo's claim that she planned to take her heart pill and head straight to bed, she would probably still be awake, waiting up for him much the same way she had when he was a teenager out on a date. Although this time the date in question would be coming home with him and sleeping under the same roof. But that wasn't the only reason he felt so restless at the moment, or why going back to the condo and the possibility of more conversation with his grandmother held little appeal.

He was thinking about what Elizabeth had said. She was right, of course. He had used the deepening feelings of the women he'd dated as the gauge for how soon to end things. He'd thought he was doing them both a favor that way. He'd certainly ensured that his heart remained whole and his head clear.

So, how was it possible than in a very short span of time, Elizabeth had managed to get under his skin?

If I were to let myself fall for you...

His mind kept working its way back to that phrase. It had him terrified even as it tempted him. He wasn't falling in love, he assured himself, but he couldn't ignore that his footing was far from sure.

"It's a pretty night," Elizabeth commented as they stepped outside the restaurant.

Overhead, the moon was nearly full, the sky awash in stars and the night air scented with flowers. He decided to follow Nana Jo's advice.

"What do you say we go for a walk?" When she hesitated he added, "You can work off those two pathetically small bites of my cake that you had."

"Don't forget my dessert."

"A handful of berries and that sliver of tartlet, you mean?" He chuckled, hoping to lighten the mood that had grown as heavy as the red velvet cake. "I told you you'd wind up leaving most of it on your plate."

"No one likes a know-it-all, Thomas. Trust me on that."

When she frowned, he reached for her hand. "You're thinking of your brother now."

It came as a surprise to realize how much he wanted to be her sounding board, her confidante, and to take away that line of dismay creasing her brow.

"I think of him every day."

"Have you thought of asking your parents for his contact information and calling him to clear the air?"

"Yes. And I have. But he doesn't stay put long enough."

"What about hiring a private investigator to locate him?"

"I've considered that, too." She sighed. "I'm not sure what it would accomplish, though. He's made it plain through his continued silence that he doesn't want anything to do with me."

Thomas wasn't sure he agreed, but he decided to let the subject drop for now. "Come on. Let's take that walk. You can point out the rest of my deficiencies while we're on the beach. There's a nice stretch of it that's open to the public not too far from my grandmother's condo."

They reached his car, and he opened the door for her. She waited for him to do so this time. He used the opportunity to lean closer and inhale.

"What are you doing?" she asked.

"Torturing myself." And then he kissed her.

He drove to a public lot with access to a stretch of Lake Michigan shoreline. During the day it was dotted with families. This time of evening, it was largely deserted, although a handful of high school kids had made a bonfire and were huddled around it laughing and talking.

Since walking on sand was best accomplished in bare feet, they both took off their shoes. He left his jacket and tie in the car as well, rolling up the sleeves of his shirt just as he had the legs of his pants.

Under his feet, the sand felt cool. The water, he knew, would be cold. Even during the hottest days of summer, the lake remained chilly. Knowing that helped cool some of his ardor when he reached for her hand again. In a friendly tone, he said, "So, shoot. Floor's all yours. As promised, this is your opportunity to rake me over the coals."

"I can't think of anything."

He squeezed her fingers. "My ego thanks you, but I think you're just being polite."

She pulled her hand away, ostensibly to

rescue her hair from the breeze. She gathered the wayward strands behind her nape before letting it fall free. She didn't reach for his hand again afterward. Distance. The weekend wasn't even over and she was already slipping away from him.

"You know all about being polite. And that's not a complaint, by the way. I like your manners. I mean, what woman wouldn't?"

He frowned momentarily at her mention of other women, again. He didn't want them brought into their conversation. "Since you can't think of anything bad to say about me, maybe you could just list the many things you find so appealing."

He meant it to be a joke. She remained serious.

"I do find you appealing, Thomas. And there are a number of reasons for that. I think you can figure out most of them. Surely, I wouldn't be the first woman to comment on your overall attractiveness."

His frustration grew. He stopped walking, turned and grasped her arms. "That's a stingy compliment. And I'll tell you something else I don't appreciate." Even in the dim light he saw her eyelids flicker in surprise at his impatient tone. "It's no great secret that I've dated other women, but I prefer not to have them brought up right now. I'm not out with them, Elizabeth. I'm with you."

It was the wrong thing to say. He knew that even as the breeze snatched away the last of his words. "Don't say it," he warned.

"Okay, but I think we're fooling ourselves. We're not together, Thomas." She shook her head sadly. "Not even close."

The teens up the beach set off a couple of fountain fireworks. Multicolored sparks shot a dozen feet into the air before raining down. A much bigger, professionally put-together fireworks display was scheduled for the following evening off Beaver Island in Lake Michigan. He and Elizabeth would be back downstate by then. Back to their separate, colorless lives.

Love has a way of finding us, Tommy. Even if we never look. Maybe especially when we don't.

Nana Jo's words whispered in his head, and he jolted as if a stray spark had landed on his skin.

"Thomas?"

"I think we'd better go back."

"Now who's the one with regrets," Elizabeth said softly.

He was, Thomas thought. But he wasn't at all sure they were the regrets she meant.

* * *

Nana Jo wasn't up when they got back. A lamp illuminated the empty living room, where she'd once again set out a blanket, sheet and pillow on the couch for Thomas.

"Well, good night," Elizabeth said.

"Let me walk you to your door."

The door in question belonged to the bedroom. She turned at the threshold. "What time will we be leaving in the morning?"

"I'm in no rush." When he attempted to tuck the hair behind her ear, she stepped back. "Apparently you are."

"Things are getting…too complicated."

Something he had been careful to steer clear of in the past. He nodded in agreement. "When we get back to Ann Arbor, maybe we could—"

"No." She shook her head. "That wouldn't be a good idea. It's called self-preservation, Thomas. Ultimately, you and I are after vastly different things from a relationship."

"Is that what you want from me? A real and committed relationship?" It was a thrilling, if terrifying thought.

Her smile was sad. "I want love, Thomas, unconditional and lasting, and I want all of the pretty promises that go with it. And, ultimately, I want to stand in a church and take vows. My parents have never done that.

They've always said they don't need a ceremony and piece of paper. But I do. That's something I need with the man who loves me."

He swallowed. "Elizabeth, I don't know if I can—"

She put a hand over his lips to silence him. "I know. You spelled that out in capital letters from the start. I'm the one who hasn't been clear on what I want, in part because I didn't think it mattered or that *you* would come to matter the way that you have. I love you, Thomas."

Her eyes rounded as if she hadn't intended to make that admission. If it surprised her, it shocked him to his core. More than that, it scared him. He could picture clearly his father the day of his mother's funeral. Hoyt had thrown himself on the casket after the church service.

I want to go with her. I can't live without her, his father had shrieked as Thomas looked on.

Now he was looking at Elizabeth and feeling almost as lost and desperate as his father had all those years ago.

"Does it help if I tell you that you're the first woman I've ever met who makes me question the decision I made?"

She rose on tiptoe and kissed his cheek.

"In a way, that makes it worse," she said and then closed the door.

CHAPTER THIRTEEN

"ANOTHER cup of coffee?"

Mel stood in the door of her office. It had been more than two weeks since Elizabeth had returned from Charlevoix. Thomas had dropped her at her door, thanked her and bid her goodbye. She hadn't heard from him since, unless one counted the check that had arrived. It was drafted from his personal bank account and was a couple thousand dollars more than what they had discussed.

Guilt money, she decided. And, as tempted as she'd been to rip it up, she'd deposited it. At least Literacy Liaisons would benefit from her utter stupidity.

She'd told Thomas she wouldn't lie. Well, she had. She'd lied to herself. And she'd done such a bang-up job of it that, despite the clear picture he'd drawn for her to the contrary, she'd almost started to believe she could have the fairy tale. As she'd told Thomas their last night in Charlevoix, it was worse knowing she was the first woman who had him second-guessing his no-commitment stance. She'd admitted she loved him. If that wasn't enough to change his mind…

"No more coffee for me. Any more and my heart is going to bounce out of my chest," she told her friend.

"Well, you might want to hang on to it. Thomas is here to see you."

Her friend stepped away, giving Elizabeth only a couple of minutes to get her head around the idea that he'd come to see her. She smoothed down her hair, mussed it up and then, irritated with herself, smoothed it down once more just as a tap sounded at her door.

"Come in."

"Hi."

He smiled uncertainly from the doorway. The heart she'd convinced herself wasn't even close to being broken cracked a little just at the sight of him.

"Hi."

"I hope I'm not bothering you."

Bothering her? No. Killing her more like. But she managed a smile, and motioned with her hand. "Not at all. Come in, please."

He entered the office, but he didn't take a

seat. The fact that he looked nervous helped calm Elizabeth's jittering pulse.

"I was going to call. I've been meaning to since we returned from Charlevoix, but—"

"I know. It's okay." For the best even, or so she'd spent long hours during the past two weeks of sleepless nights trying to convince herself. "I got your check, by the way."

"And I got your thank-you note."

"Right. The amount, it was kind of you."

"As you said in the card. It was the least I could do."

They eyed one another uncomfortably for a moment. "Is there, um, a reason for your unexpected visit today?" she asked. *Other than torture.*

"There is." He grimaced. "I've come to ask another favor."

Her heart sank. For just a moment she'd let herself hope… "What do you need?"

"Some more of your time. Nana Jo has invited us back up for the Venetian Festival on Lake Charlevoix this coming weekend."

"Thomas—"

"Just hear me out, please." At her nod, he said, "We'll stay at the bed-and-breakfast, no ifs, ands or buts, this time. And we'll leave the following morning. Barely twenty-four hours of your time, Elizabeth, that's all I'm asking."

"You're asking for a lot more than that," she said quietly.

He nodded and had the grace to flush. "I know. Believe me, I wouldn't put you in this position if it wasn't a matter of life and death."

She frowned at that. "Nana Jo?"

"I've been in touch with a doctor. It's a heart issue," he said slowly.

"Are you sure?" Elizabeth certainly wasn't. The woman was as healthy as they came, and Thomas was hardly objective where she was concerned.

But his expression was serious, somber, when he replied, "Positive. It's definitely a heart issue. And, from what I've been told, it's not going to change. In fact, it's likely to get worse."

"I'm so sorry. Of course, I'll come."

It was late Saturday afternoon when they arrived in Charlevoix. As much as Elizabeth wanted to do this for Nana Jo's sake, it was costing her. Every smile, every glance Thomas sent her way in the car landed like daggers. Twenty-four hours, she reminded herself. Twenty-four hours and she would be back home where she could start for the second time the process of getting over him.

Or maybe she would just kill him, she decided, when a rosy-cheeked Nana Jo opened the condo door after the third knock.

"Sorry, I didn't hear you. I was 'Sweatin' to the Oldies' with Richard Simmons."

Elizabeth rounded on Thomas. "Her heart? A matter of life and death? How dare you!" Before storming away, she told Nana Jo, "I'm sorry. So sorry. But I can't stay. I won't."

As Thomas turned to follow her, his grandmother put a hand on his arm to stop him.

"Give her a minute, Tommy."

"This was a bad idea."

"I don't think so. She loves you."

"She's ready to kill me."

"Takes love to stir up an emotion that strong," she assured him.

Nana Jo smiled. In a phone call after their last visit, she'd confronted him about the true nature of his relationship with Elizabeth, taking great delight in the fact that he was every bit as smitten as he'd pretended to be.

"Love takes courage," she'd told him. She said the same thing again now.

"How long am I supposed to give her?" he asked, glancing at his watch as Nana Jo sipped from her water bottle, not a care in the world. "It's been five minutes."

She smiled knowingly. "I guess that's long enough. Go." He was at the door when he heard her delighted laughter. "Don't forget to get down on one knee."

He caught up with Elizabeth on the beach. The waves pounded the shore. A storm was brewing. How apropos, he thought as emotions crashed around inside of him.

"If you even come near me…" she warned.

He held up his hands. "Let me explain."

"You told me it was her heart!" she accused.

"Actually, I never said whose heart I was referring to."

She stopped walking, frowned at him. "A doctor. I distinctly recall the mention of a doctor."

"I said I'd been in touch with one, yes. Mine. My heart, Elizabeth." He liked the way her mouth formed an *O*. It took his mind off his nerves, gave him the courage to press ahead. "The doctor couldn't find a thing wrong with me despite this persistent ache I've been having right here." He took her hand, flattened its palm against his chest.

"Thomas?"

"I've diagnosed it myself. A chronic condition, I'm afraid." He grew serious now. "Elizabeth, I can't live without you. But I will. I won't climb into a bottle like my father and drink the rest of my life away if you're not in it. But I will feel an acute sense of loss, because I know just how much better my life could be with you in it."

"I don't know what to say."

"I was hoping for 'I love you.' The last time you said it, I wasn't ready to hear it, but I am now. I just hope you haven't changed your mind."

It seemed an eternity that he waited for her smile to blossom, her arms to slip around his neck. "I love you, Thomas Waverly."

He crushed her to his chest on a laugh that was part sob. "Thank God! I was worried I'd lost you."

"I was worried you might never find your way back to me."

"I won't make that mistake again."

He did as his grandmother suggested, going down on one knee in front of Elizabeth in the sand.

"Oh, my," he heard her murmur from behind the hand that covered her mouth.

This ring wasn't the one his father had given his mother. Too much history was attached to that one, Thomas had decided. Too many sad memories. He wanted a fresh start for the new life he wanted to make with the woman he loved, although not necessarily a new ring.

"This was Nana Jo's engagement ring," he said of the half-carat, brilliant-cut solitaire. "She and my grandfather had nearly four decades of happiness together before he died. She sent it to me via overnight post last week when we hatched this plan." His grin faltered then. "Elizabeth, will you marry me?"

"I will. Yes." She laughed as she wiped away a tear. "In fact, I thought you'd never ask."

EPILOGUE

Six months later

"HOWIE, stop!" Elizabeth shouted as the dog started down the street after the mail truck. "Come back here now!"

He reluctantly obeyed. They were going to have to see about installing one of those invisible fences at Thomas's home. Their home, she corrected on a grin.

She and Thomas had just returned from their honeymoon—two of the most blissful weeks of her life on the big island of Hawaii.

"I see the mail came," Thomas remarked, moving in behind her. He nuzzled her neck, sending her pulse racing. She wondered if she'd ever get used to his touch.

"Lots of junk and bills," she said, starting to flip through the huge stack that had accumulated while they were gone. "Oh, here's a card from Nana Jo." She handed it to him to open, while she continued through the pile of letters.

Thomas's laughter had her glancing over curiously. "What is it?"

"She's wanting to know when we're going to give her great-grandchildren. She's not as young as she used to be, you know. She's been feeling a little peaked since our wedding."

Elizabeth laughed too until the writing on one of the envelopes caught her attention. It was childlike and all in uppercase letters. "What on earth…"

"Open it," Thomas said quietly. "Go on."

She did and started to read the simple words only to have her eyes blur with tears. "Ross…" she sobbed.

"I found him for you, Elizabeth. A couple months ago, in fact."

"Why didn't you say something before now?" she asked, her head bursting with questions, her heart bursting with emotion.

"He wasn't able to come to our wedding, and he made me promise not to say anything until he could contact you himself. With a letter." Thomas smiled. "He's been taking night classes at a men's shelter in Seattle."

"He's learning how to read and write."

Thomas nodded and took the letter from her hands. He read the rest of it for her as tears streamed down her cheeks. Ross wasn't only learning how to read and write. He was coming home, back to Michigan. Back to her life.

"I want you to be as proud of me as I am of you. I love you, Lizzie." It was right there, spelled out in his awkward and perfect penmanship.

"Oh, Thomas," she said, pulling her new husband close. The rest of the envelopes fell from her hands and scattered over the floor. "Thank you. Thank you. You've made me so happy."

The embrace lasted, grew more intimate.

He pulled back with a wicked grin. "So, what do you say we go try to make Nana Jo happy and fulfill her great-grandbabies request?"

Elizabeth offered her own wicked smile, grasped his hand and started to lead the way to their bedroom.

"This could take a while."

* * * * *

A sneaky peek at next month...

RIVA™

LIVE LIFE TO THE FULL – GIVE IN TO TEMPTATION

My wish list for next month's titles...

In stores from 4th May 2012:

❑ Never Stay Past Midnight – Mira Lyn Kelly

❑ One Day to Find a Husband – Shirley Jump

❑ The Last Woman He'd Ever Date – Liz Fielding

Available at WHSmith, Tesco, Asda, Eason, Amazon and Apple

Just can't wait?

Visit us Online

You can buy our books online a month before they hit the shops! **www.millsandboon.co.uk**

0412/06

Book of the Month

MILLS & BOON

We love this book because...

Rafe St Alban is the most dark-hearted, sinfully attractive rake in London. So get ready for fireworks when he sweeps prim Miss Henrietta Markham off her feet in Marguerite Kaye's compellingly sensual story of redemption!

On sale 4th May

Visit us Online

Find out more at
www.millsandboon.co.uk/BOTM

0412/BOTM

MILLS & BOON Book Club — *2 Free Books!*

Join the Mills & Boon Book Club

Want to read more **Riva**™
books? We're offering
you **2 more** absolutely **FREE!**

We'll also treat you to these fabulous extras:

- Books up to 2 months ahead of shops

- FREE home delivery

- Bonus books with our special rewards scheme

- Exclusive offers and much more!

Get your free books now!

Visit us Online — Find out more at
www.millsandboon.co.uk/freebookoffer

SUBS/ONLINE/R

Special Offers

Every month we put together collections and longer reads written by your favourite authors.

Here are some of next month's highlights— and don't miss our fabulous discount online!

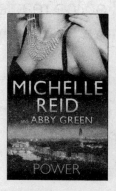

On sale 20th April   On sale 20th April   On sale 20th April

Save 20% on all Special Releases

Find out more at
www.millsandboon.co.uk/specialreleases

Visit us Online

0412/ST/MB369

Mills & Boon® Online

Discover more romance at
www.millsandboon.co.uk

- ❧ **FREE** online reads
- ❧ **Books** up to one month before shops
- ❧ **Browse our books** before you buy

...and much more!

For exclusive competitions and instant updates:

 Like us on **facebook.com/romancehq**

 Follow us on **twitter.com/millsandboonuk**

 Join us on **community.millsandboon.co.uk**

Visit us Online | Sign up for our FREE eNewsletter at **www.millsandboon.co.uk**

WEB/M&B/RTL4

Have Your Say

You've just finished your book.
So what did you think?

We'd love to hear your thoughts on our
'Have your say' online panel
www.millsandboon.co.uk/haveyoursay

- 🌹 Easy to use
- 🌹 Short questionnaire
- 🌹 Chance to win Mills & Boon® goodies

Visit us Online

Tell us what you thought of this book now at
www.millsandboon.co.uk/haveyoursay

YOUR_SAY